BLOOD AND WATER

Briana Morgan

ISBN: 1544170610
ISBN-13: 978-1544170619

Edited by Sarah Macklin
Cover design by Johannus Steger
Interior layout by Coryl Addy

For my grandfather, who instilled in me a love for telling stories.

Chapter One

BLOOD IN THE SINK

There was blood in the sink. That wasn't unusual. But Jay hadn't been home all day, so it couldn't have been his. That was the furthest thing from usual.

He reached down to scratch behind Samson's ears. The fat, orange cat was purring. That meant there couldn't be an intruder in the apartment, right? Did cats even care if intruders broke in, like dogs, or were they apathetic about that, too?

Samson was apathetic about everything but food and ear scratches.

"Hello?" Jay ventured.

No response. Of course not. What had he expected, someone to jump out and go *boo*? Melanie would say he'd seen too many horror movies. Sean would argue maybe he hadn't seen enough. As much as they loved each other, they seldom agreed. Still, besides the homeless people, they were all he had.

He had just gotten home from his volunteer shift at the homeless shelter on the other side of the river. Although its numbers had dwindled, they were still in desperate need of volunteers. Many people had stopped volunteering, worried about catching the virus, but Jay still went as much as he could. Immunity had done wonders for his compassion.

Immunity. His mouth twitched.

Jay had been helping out there since moving to London three years before. He'd been thinking about how much things had changed and trying to fill a glass with water from the sink when he looked down and saw the blood. He'd been coughing up a lot of blood lately, but where had this stuff come from?

Samson meowed. Jay stooped to pet him. The cat purred as though nothing had happened while Jay was gone. Useless.

"Was someone here?" he asked Samson.

The cat blinked in response. Jay would have to investigate the apartment himself.

Samson rubbed against Jay's jeans before venturing down the hallway.

Jay peered down at the blood in the kitchen sink. *Dark, thick, red.* He went to the drawer in search of a knife.

In a world racked with disease, it was hard to imagine crime was still an issue. Ebola-II, as it had been dubbed, was an absolute nightmare virus—everyone agreed on that. Tragedy was supposed to band people together. Why kick one person when the whole world was down? Still, there were riots. People got murdered almost every day. The week before, he'd seen someone get stabbed right outside of Hyde Park. Jay wished he'd had a weapon to protect himself. Luckily, the killer hadn't come after Jay—he took the man's wallet and ran into a tunnel.

In the present, Jay's reflection was a flash of brown skin on the blade of the knife. He had his mother's skin, smoother and lighter than his father's. On her, it had been beautiful. It made Jay look soft. His rounded jawline and warm brown eyes didn't do much for his intimidation factor, either. The only part of his face that was sharp was his nose. In the context of his face, it almost made no sense. It was his father's nose, and whenever he saw it, he was forced to remember his parents were dead.

Jay inhaled through his teeth. His close-cropped hair bristled as though it wanted to leave his scalp. It wasn't the best feeling. After a minute, he wiped his sweaty palms on his thighs, and then he closed his fingers around the black rubber handle.

Time to search for the intruder.

He tried to think of all the reasons someone would break into his apartment. He didn't live on the wealthy side of town, and there was nothing outside his door to suggest he had any money.

He didn't even have a television, for God's sake. In his wallet, which he couldn't be bothered to keep on his person, there was a ten-pound note and a couple of coins. Then again, money wasn't much good anymore. Commerce had been annihilated by the virus, and most people still working in the shops didn't care if you took something without paying. Theft was the least of their worries.

The wallet rested on his nightstand. If the intruder had made it into the bedroom and picked up the wallet, they were bound to have laughed.

Samson rubbed against Jay's legs again as he walked through the living room. If he listened, he couldn't hear anything out of the ordinary—just the stillness of the apartment and the sleeping city beyond it. He'd lived in London pre-plague—all commotion, no rest. It was impossible to believe now. He almost couldn't remember a life without a curfew, let alone one in which people swarmed the streets, even though he'd experienced London's busyness once himself.

Before the plague, it was impossible to get anywhere during rush hour. If you tried to ride the Underground, even to the South Bank, you were going to be delayed. Even if you weren't delayed, you'd be packed into a train car with a hundred other people. You could spend a whole ride with your nose in someone's armpit or your hand against the door, trapped there by someone's buttocks.

Back in the present, Jay opened the coat closet by the door, knife poised for action. With his right hand, he pushed the coats aside.

Nothing. A wave of relief broke over him.

Still, he had more of the apartment to explore. The two-bedroom rental had been Maia's when Jay first moved to London. They'd lived there together for a while. Then, Maia moved in with a boyfriend somewhere near Shepherd's Bush. The boyfriend had died, Jay couldn't remember how long ago. Maia still lived in the apartment they'd shared. Jay's place in Bexley was modest and far enough from the city proper to be fairly quiet. Then again, in the wake of the virus, *everywhere* was quiet.

It wasn't a large space—two bedrooms, a kitchen, a bathroom, and a meager living room—but it now felt cavernous. He crossed the linoleum of the kitchen and stopped at the edge of the carpeted hallway. Fears of the unknown swirled in his head, magnifying the apartment's interior. The more he thought about how much he still had to search, the worse he felt. Instead, he tried to focus on the feeling of the knife.

Jay drew in a shaky breath and started down the hallway. The charity-store furniture in the living room fell out of his sight. What he hadn't gotten cheap had been free—hand-me-down items and castoffs from his friends. Normally, the sight of the items comforted him. In the fading sunlight, it was difficult to see. Everything cast eerie shadows on the walls, obscuring corners of the apartment. But he didn't want to risk turning on the lights for fear of alerting the intruder.

Then again, hadn't he called out right after getting home?

Idiot.

Samson padded down the hallway past Jay, oblivious to the threat of danger. The cat was safe, Jay knew. Whoever had broken into his home meant to harm him, not his pet. With any luck, the intruder would adopt Samson after killing Jay. It was the least he could do, all things considered.

His life could be in danger, and he was worried about the cat. What was wrong with him?

Right after he'd moved to London, following in Maia's footsteps, she'd brought him the cat as a housewarming gift. Their father had been allergic to most animals, and Jay had always wanted a pet of his own. Maia chose a cat because they were low maintenance. If Jay couldn't remember to buy new milk before the old milk spoiled, there was no way in hell he could handle a dog. Then again, it wasn't as if he'd moved into an empty place—Maia would be there to take care of any pet they got, too, but she wouldn't hear another word. As much as he wanted to argue more, there hadn't been a need. Samson was everything he wanted in a pet—minus

8

the lack of protection, of course. Then again, he'd never been in a situation like this before. There had been no need for him to yearn for protection.

Jay tightened his grip on the knife. He pushed the thought away. *Focus.*

A noise in the bedroom at the end of the hall made him freeze in his tracks. The floorboards creaked. He flattened his back against the wall and stood still for a minute, straining to hear any sounds of life. The silence made his ears ring.

Then, somebody coughed.

Jay clapped a hand over his mouth, not wanting to give himself away, but his throat wasn't burning. He lowered his hand, examining his fingers. No blood. His chest felt loose, too. He hadn't coughed.

The intruder. He should have known—the virus wasn't picky.

The floorboards in the bedroom creaked again as the intruder moved.

Whoever had broken into the apartment was sick because half the world was sick. It made perfect, maddening sense.

Jay swallowed hard against a wave of nausea lined with fear. At one point, contracting the virus had scared him more than the thought of getting killed. Now that he had the virus, well, it wasn't the worst thing that could happen. Basic human instinct gave him several other options.

As Jay got closer to the bedroom, there was blood spattered on the carpet. It had dripped from the intruder. He'd lost a lot of blood, more than Jay had expected.

The bedroom door was ajar. Jay nudged it with his toe.

The knife glinted as he flipped on the lights. No one was there. Jay stood in the doorway for a minute, puzzled. He'd heard somebody moving around.

Light emanated from underneath the bathroom door. Jay took a step forward.

Squish. He froze.

What the hell had he stepped on?

Blood pooled dark and thick on the carpet at his feet. It was similar in texture to the blood in the sink. There was a trail leading from it to the bathroom. He raised the knife, stepped forward, and opened the bathroom door.

His older sister, Maia, was hunched over the white sink, retching. A string of saliva stretched from her mouth. When she turned to face Jay, she had blood on her chin. Her skin, normally a half shade darker than his, was paler than he'd ever seen it. Her hazel eyes were red rimmed and swollen, glistening with tears. Her natural hair was a disaster—she'd pulled it into a ponytail but several coils had fallen out to rest against her face.

He dropped the knife. "Maia? What's going on?"

"Jay," she said. "Thank God."

"How did you get in here?"

"You never changed the locks." She wiped her mouth with the back of her hand. "I didn't know where else to go."

"You walked here?"

"Does it matter?"

Jay's stomach lurched. "How long?"

"A week ago." She looked into the sink. "I'm sorry. I should have called you."

Jay leaned against the wall. His shoulders slumped. One week. Their parents had been dead in four. The less he thought about the time frame, the better.

"Why didn't you tell me?"

"I don't know," she said. "I didn't want to scare you."

She hadn't wanted to scare him. That was typical Maia. Typical of both of them, really. Tears ran down her face, and her lower lip trembled. Her eyes were bloodshot with dark circles pillowed beneath them. Blood spattered her shirt.

"Jesus," Jay said. "You need help."

Maia coughed and spit something else into the sink. She wiped her mouth again. "No one here can help me."

"We'll go somewhere else, then. We'll find you a doctor."

Jay tried to think of some lead he hadn't followed yet. He'd been all over London in search of a cure. Nothing had turned up. He was running out of time.

"Doesn't matter," she said.

"Course it does," Jay answered.

Maia turned on the tap, cupped water in her hands, and splashed it on her face. Some of it dripped off her chin and landed on her chest. "I'm so glad you're immune to this."

"Yeah," Jay said, "me, too."

He'd been sick for three weeks. She would never find out.

Chapter Two

THREE IN THE MORNING

Maia cried herself to sleep that night.

Jay couldn't sleep at all.

He gave Maia his bed and lay down on the couch. He tossed and turned for two hours before giving up and going into the kitchen. After feeding Samson, he poured himself a glass of water. It tasted like metal.

Jay needed sleep. He hadn't slept in ages. Wasn't sleep supposed to strengthen your immune system? Not that it mattered. He was already sick.

Now, so was Maia. What were they going to do?

Jay had spent the past few weeks looking for a cure. It was like Maia said—there was no help in London. He wondered if they would've been safer if they'd stayed in Chicago. He couldn't spend time dwelling on the *what ifs*. It had been Maia's decision to move to London and his to follow her. The virus was everywhere, and it had spread fast. Perhaps they never would have been able to avoid it.

Jay needed to tell his sister he was sick, too. Every time he thought about it, he felt like throwing up—and not because of the virus. Maia thought he was immune. He worked with contaminated people and hadn't gotten sick—but that was before the virus hit London. Once it touched the island, no one was safe. It had taken a while to get to Jay, but the minute he sneezed, it was over. If he went to the doctor, he'd be quarantined. They'd separate him from everyone he loved, and they wouldn't be able to see him anymore. Even if he died, they wouldn't get to see the body—every sick person ended up cremated, after all.

He couldn't risk it. There was no way they were going to take him away from Maia. They were all each other had. He refused to lose her, too.

At three in the morning, he called his friend Sean. Of course, there was no answer. Sean was fast asleep.

He didn't know Jay was sick, either. Jay was too afraid to tell Sean—he wanted to keep his friend around, even though there was a chance Sean would catch the virus. He avoided Sean as much as he could, but he didn't have the courage to sever the connection.

If anything happened to Sean, he'd never forgive himself.

Unable to reach Sean, Jay called Melanie McCartney, Sean's girlfriend. He'd been the one to introduce them. Sean's eyes had lit up when he shook Melanie's hand. They'd been inseparable since. Jay had known Melanie since moving to London. He adored her. It helped that he loved Sean, too. Whenever the three of them hung out, Jay was never a third wheel. They were a trio.

Melanie picked up on the third ring, voice thick with sleep. "What's wrong?"

"Why do you think something's wrong?" Jay asked.

"The last time you called this late, Samson was choking."

Jay looked over at the cat. Still eating. "I just need somebody to talk to."

"I'll be over in ten. Could you put the kettle on?"

Jay smiled. "No problem."

He could always count on Melanie to cheer him up. She was the only other person who knew he was sick. He hadn't wanted her to know, but she'd walked in on him vomiting the previous week, and that was that. She knew.

The only good thing was that she didn't treat him differently. If anything, she spent more time around him than she had before, even knowing she could catch the virus. She cared that much about him.

Jay picked up the electric kettle and turned on the faucet.

As he set the kettle in the sink, a sharp pain knifed his ribs. He clutched at his sides and doubled over, swearing. The pain was new. His vision darkened.

What was happening to him?

He sank to his knees on the hard tile. Whatever was going on, it was terrifying. Cold sweat beaded on his forehead and dripped down his face. He was in agony. It was one thing to know the pain was coming, but it had come out of nowhere. His parents had been in so much pain. Was this what it had been like in the end? Had it gotten worse for them?

Saliva clogged his throat. He could *not* puke in the kitchen.

Closing his eyes, Jay rocked back on his heels and waited. If he didn't move, maybe he could will away the nausea. His eyelids were hot. Not a good sign. He swallowed what he hoped wasn't bile or blood. Something was going to have to come up at some point.

It took all his strength to stand. Once he was upright again, all the blood rushed out of his head and everything went dark. If he hadn't grabbed the counter, he would've collapsed. Since when had standing become an ordeal?

He got worse with each passing day. How much longer did he have?

Toward the end, his father hadn't recognized him, his only son, his *baby*. The forgetfulness scared Jay more than anything else. The bleeding and pain were to be expected. The memory loss was a slap in the face.

Jay shuddered hard. His eyes flew open. Had someone knocked on the door?

He held his breath, listening to the stillness in the air.

After a minute, the noise came again: *knock knock knock.*

Then, there was a voice.

"Jay," Melanie said, "it's me. Open up."

An immense relief flooded Jay's veins. Melanie fixed every-thing. She was the levelheaded one—all practical knowledge with the right amount of heart to keep from seeming smug. He took a deep breath and headed toward the door. Every step spanned a century. Why was he so sluggish?

He needed Melanie. She would help him.

When he opened the door, she smiled. As she looked him over, though, the smile faded. "Arsehole. You never said you were having an episode. I would've come here straightaway."

"I'm not having an episode."

"Liar. Look at you."

Jay winced. The pain in his sides cut into his stomach. Something was wrong, no doubt about it. Something far beyond the normal level of awful. Fear etched lines in Melanie's face.

"I've felt better."

"Bet you have," she said. "Can I come inside or what?"

Melanie pushed past Jay without waiting for a response. She went straight to the kitchen, got out a glass, and filled it at the sink. Jay followed her.

After he sat at the table, she handed him the water. "Drink up. You're dehydrated."

"How can you tell?"

"You don't drink enough. Never have. I know you, Jaybird."

He flushed. "You haven't called me that in a long time."

A smile quirked her lips. "I'm sorry."

Jay wasn't sure whether she was apologizing for calling him that or for not calling him that in such a long time. Either way, she had nothing to be sorry for. His chest tightened.

"I need to tell you something. It's about my sister."

"Oh."

She poured herself a glass of water and sat in the chair next to Jay. She stared into the glass rather than meeting his eyes. Maybe she knew what he was going to say. She had gotten good at reading his mind.

"Drink," she said.

Jay looked at his glass. The thought of drinking it repulsed him.

He blamed the virus.

"I had some before you came."

"For the love of God."

He sighed, shoulders slumping, and downed the contents of the glass in a single gulp. When he set the empty cup down, Melanie was staring at him.

"Just say it," she said.

"Maia is sick. She's been sick for a week. She only just told me." Melanie sucked in a shaky breath.

"I'm sorry," he said.

"I should be saying that to you."

They sat in solemn silence. Tears dripped down Melanie's face. More than anything, Jay yearned to reassure her, but there was nothing he could tell her. Besides, he needed someone to reassure him, too.

All he could think to do was put his arms around Melanie. He leaned closer to her and did just that. She melted into him. There was nothing left to say.

"She doesn't know, then."

Maybe Melanie meant the sentence as a question, but it came out as a statement. Maybe she didn't want an answer, but validation for what she suspected.

"She will never know," he answered.

He wanted to spare Maia the pain of what he felt when he thought about losing her. They'd come through losing two parents, but barely. The less they thought about losing each other, the better off they'd be. Right? And surely Melanie understood that. Melanie *always* understood.

Melanie opened her mouth to speak.

Whatever she said was completely eclipsed by the pain in Jay's abdomen. It flared up and stabbed him. He cried out.

"What's wrong? Your stomach?"

Jay couldn't speak. The pain was incredible.

"Should we go to hospital?"

"No," Jay said. "Never."

"You might be dying."

"I know."

He threw up on the tile. The vomit was dark and there was blood in it—*dark, thick, red*—so much like Maia's that he threw up again. Before he knew it, he was crying. His face was hot, his throat burned, and he was crying. When he looked up, so was Melanie.

"I'm scared," she said.

"Me, too."

"Do you want me to call Sean?"

"Tried that. He was sleeping."

Melanie put her feet on the chair and pulled her knees to her chest. "What are we going to do for you two? We need to find a doctor."

"I'm not going to the hospital. You know what they'll do."

"We might be out of options."

"There must be someone out there with some kind of cure. Billions of people have died already, and more people are dying every day. There are scientists trying to stop it." He shook his head. "Otherwise… what's the point?"

She wiped her face. "What?"

"If humanity is doomed, maybe I'll just shoot myself."

"Damn it. Don't say that."

"Why not?" His voice rose, bordering on furious. "I'm dying. Why can't I go on my terms?"

"You're breaking my heart." She was so pale he could almost see through her skin. Her pallor made the freckles stand out on her cheeks. Melanie was beautiful. Somehow, he'd forgotten. She was his friend. She was also Sean's girlfriend. And of course, she'd been crying. He shouldn't stare at her.

"Melanie," he said.

Water droplets hung suspended in her eyelashes. He reached out and brushed one out of the way. Melanie kept her eyes closed, even when he pulled away. His entire body ached for her. He wanted to kiss her more than anything.

Her eyes flew open. "Thank you. Still hurting?"

"It's bearable."

Without asking for permission, he grabbed the glass in front of her and swallowed all the water. He was about to get up and get more when he noticed movement out of the corner of his eye.

Maia stood at the edge of the kitchen, eyes wide in horror as she looked at the vomit.

"Who's sick?" she asked.

Chapter Three

THE LIST

"I am," Melanie said. "Just found out this week."

Maia stood there, blinking, as though she didn't understand.

Panic registered in the back of Jay's mind. Melanie was dying. He mentally shook himself—no, she wasn't dying. She wasn't even sick. She was just doing everything she could to protect his sister from finding out what was happening to him.

But Maia didn't know that.

Jay expected his sister to burst into tears. He pictured her face crumpling and her shoulders shaking with sobs. None of those things happened. Maia went over to the pantry, took out the bag of flour, and poured it on the vomit. She dropped the empty bag in the trashcan.

"I'm going back to bed," she said.

"Maia," Melanie said, "do you—"

"Going back to sleep."

Melanie started after her, but Jay caught her wrist. "Let her go."

Once Maia was gone, the two of them settled back in their seats. Jay tapped his fingers on the table. He wasn't sure whether to thank Melanie. In one way, she'd saved him. In another, she'd made things worse. Now, Maia thought her friend was dying. How would she react once she learned that Jay was sick?

"I didn't know what else to do," Melanie said.

"I know," Jay said. "It's cool."

He got up from the table and got the broom from the closet. Although his movements were shaky, he swept the flour into a pile. Melanie grabbed the dustpan and knelt down in front of Jay.

"What are you doing?" he asked.

"Helping," she said.

"With Maia or the flour?"

"Yes. I said I'm helping."

No matter what happened, Melanie was on his side. Loyal, that one. To a *fault*. It would be her undoing. Guilt twisted his gut. She deserved his gratitude, nothing else. Despite how he felt about her methods, she had kept his secret so far—more than most people would do for him.

"Sorry if I don't sound thankful." He swept the pile of flour into the dustpan. Swirls of white flew up in the air.

She wiped a smear of flour from her cheek. "It's all right, Jaybird. I know you."

"I should thank you more often."

Melanie's face flushed. The reaction startled Jay. Had he said something wrong? He ran through the words in his head, trying to figure out what had happened. But when he looked back at Melanie, he saw she was smiling. Maybe what he said had been the furthest thing from wrong.

"Thank you," she said.

Jay picked up the dustpan and the broom and carried them over to the trashcan. He dumped the flour and set the broom and dustpan in the closet. The faint scent of vomit still hung in the air. Jay was surprised he'd noticed since he'd grown accustomed to it. He grabbed the mop and bucket from the closet and went over to the sink.

Melanie stood in front of him. "Don't worry about it. You're not feeling well."

"I'm never feeling well."

"Put the mop down."

Jay sighed. He handed the mop and bucket to Melanie.

She leaned them against the counter. "If it's the smell you're worried about, it doesn't bother me. I had some training to be a nurse, remember? I've dealt with worse."

Still, his cheeks heated. "Every time you come over, I throw up or faint. It's getting ridiculous."

Melanie shrugged. "It's worth it if I get to see you."

Jay crossed his arms. "What if you get sick?"

"I won't."

"You don't know that."

"I haven't caught it yet."

"So what?" he asked. "It can strike without warning. Look what happened to me."

"You were volunteering at the soup kitchen in spite of the warnings."

"I thought I was immune to it."

"We all thought you were," she murmured.

Jay shook his head. When he spoke again, his voice was close to a whisper. "I just don't want to lose you, too."

Melanie grabbed his hands. "You will never lose me."

She was right—not because she was always right, but because she'd proved her loyalty several times over. While he and Maia spread their parents' ashes in the Thames, Melanie waited at the end of the bridge. When it was all over, he went to her and let her put her arms around him. She'd held his hand as the three of them walked to a cafe. Sean had met them there, and it was before he and Melanie were dating. Melanie kept her fingers intertwined with Jay's even while they were eating.

The last good day after his parents died, before the virus struck again, the four of them had gone to the National Gallery to look around before the government shut the whole place down for the sake of quarantine. Melanie, whose mother had been an artist, flitted from one hall to the next in breathless ecstasy. Jay, Maia, and Sean tried to keep up, but it was difficult.

After Sean got tired of chasing his new girlfriend around, the group decided it might be best for them to separate. Melanie and Jay went one way; Sean and Maia, the other. Melanie led him to the part of the museum that focused on impressionism. They blazed past Cézanne, Renoir, and Turner. She stopped in front of a painting of sunflowers.

"Van Gogh," she said. "My favorite."

They stood in front of the painting, saying nothing. One minute, they were separate spectators. The next, their hands and souls entwined. She turned and looked at him and he got caught up in her eyes.

It had been almost impossible to keep from kissing her.

For Sean's sake, he had managed.

Now, Jay felt guilty for regretting that he hadn't kissed her there. He couldn't kiss her now because of the virus. Even just being with her put her at risk.

"What if you get sick?" he asked.

"Stop worrying about me." She kissed his cheek. "You're the one with the virus. Let's get back to you."

He shifted his weight from one foot to the other. He wanted to crack a joke in an attempt to break the tension, but nothing was funny anymore. Melanie stood there, looking at him. Maybe if he looked at her long enough, she would want to change the subject.

"Did you do what I suggested last week?" she asked.

Jay frowned. "I don't remember. What was it?"

"The list," she said. "I said you should come up with a list of things you want to see or do before you die. We both wanted to do it ages ago, but now… well, it seems like it could, uh, come in handy." She bit her lip. She was afraid she'd hurt his feelings.

He smiled to reassure her. "Yeah, I remember now. I made one."

"Can I see it?"

Jay blushed. "Um, sure. Let me go find it."

"I don't have to," she said.

"No," he said. "I want you to."

Melanie sat down at the table, folded her arms, and rested her head on them.

Jay walked to his bedroom and tiptoed around the bed. Maia

22

was fast asleep and snoring. Moonlight lit her face through the thin blinds.

Her cheeks were full; the bones in her face nowhere close to protruding. Her color was good. Her skin was bright.

She looked healthy.

It was torture to see her looking so peaceful while the virus destroyed her inside.

Jay's stomach clenched. He looked away.

The list sat at the back of his nightstand drawer. He eased the drawer out, supporting it from underneath with his free hand to keep it from squealing. His fingers found the folded paper without trying too hard. He pulled the list out and closed his hand around it. As he passed the bed again, Maia was still asleep. He shut the door on his way out and didn't relax until he heard the soft click behind him.

Back in the kitchen, Melanie's head was still down. Her eyes were closed.

Was she sleeping?

Without saying a word, Jay sat down in the chair next to her and laid the note down in front of him. He put his face in his hands. No one else had seen the list besides him. Although Melanie had suggested he make it, he had never intended to show it to her. Still, he couldn't say she couldn't read it, not after everything she'd done for him. She was even sacrificing her health to see him, for God's sake. How the hell could he say no?

In that moment, Jay remembered—he'd never put the kettle on. He'd meant to before he felt the sharp pain earlier. Then Melanie had come, and neither of them tried again. If Melanie was sleeping, she was dozing. She would wake up in a little bit. He'd have a cup of tea for her as soon as she woke up.

Jay thought about Maia as he waited for the water to boil. She wasn't having trouble sleeping, which was a good sign. He couldn't remember the last time he'd gotten a full night's sleep. The virus had him puking at regular intervals and waking up coughing during the night.

Melanie might not have been sleeping much, either, but it had nothing to do with her health. She was exhausted from worrying about Jay and Maia's parents and then Jay and now Maia. If she had to worry about anyone else, she might collapse.

Jay leaned back against the counter and put his face in his hands. He didn't want her to worry about him. He didn't want anyone to worry about him. He didn't know why, but he wasn't afraid of dying. He was more afraid of how his loved ones would react to him in his later days. How would they cope after he had passed on?

"What are you doing? Are you thinking about death?"

Jay lowered his hands.

Melanie scowled. "I just felt like you were, and it disturbed me awake. You should apologize."

Was there the hint of a smirk on her face?

"I'm making you some tea, so you should be nice to me."

"I'm risking my life. It better be some damn good tea."

She meant it as a joke, but it still stung. He turned his back on her, in part to pour water in mugs and in part to hide his face. He didn't want her thinking she'd upset him.

"I'm ready to hear your list once I've had my tea," she said. "Were you able to find it?"

"It was never lost," Jay said.

He dunked the tea bags up and down in the hot water until it turned brown. Melanie got annoyed with him when he did that—she said it didn't make a difference—but that time, she said nothing. Now that their time together was limited, she must have found it easier not to sweat the small stuff. If only Jay could adopt the same approach to the rest of his life.

When he set Melanie's cup of tea in front of her, she put her hand on top of his. Her fingers chilled his skin.

Jay didn't pull away. He put his other hand on top of hers.

"I love you," she said.

24

"I love you, too," he said. "Always have and always will."

Melanie winked. "Unless I tease you about what's on this list, of course. Come on, then. Let's hear it."

Jay set his cup down. He unfolded the paper and smoothed out the creases.

"Okay," he said, "promise me you won't laugh."

"I won't laugh," she said.

"You're lying."

"Just read."

Jay sighed, took a deep breath, and read.

Chapter Four

NEARLY DAWN

Samson jumped up on the table while Jay was reading. Jay stroked his fur without looking up from the paper. He tried to concentrate.

No matter how silly some of the items on the list seemed, they were all important to him. Maybe if he could say them with a straight face, Melanie wouldn't tease him about them.

"Learn to drive," he said, "swim in the Thames, spend the night at the British Museum, kiss someone in Paris—"

Melanie snorted. Jay ignored her and kept reading.

"Stay up all night talking with someone I love, get in a fight and win, get drunk, have s—"

He paused. "Eat an expensive French meal—"

"Wait," Melanie said. "You skipped one."

"No, I didn't."

"Yes, you did. You started to say one thing and went straight into another." She leaned forward on her elbows. "You can't do that. It's cheating."

"Says who?" he asked.

"Says me. Go back to where you were."

Jay folded the note up into a neat square. "Never mind the list. This was stupid, anyway."

Melanie tried to snatch the note out of his hand, but he jerked it away from her. When she got out of her chair, he leaped up and clutched the paper to his chest.

There was no way she was reading it. He'd die before that happened.

"Jay," she whined, "just let me see it."

"No," he said. "It's over."

Samson jumped down from the table and rubbed against Jay's shins. He took a step backward, away from Melanie. Samson darted past him. Melanie took a step forward.

"Jaybird," she said.

"I told you not to laugh and you laughed anyway," he said.

"No, I didn't."

"Yes, you did. You laughed when I said the thing about Paris."

"Okay, okay," she said. "I'm sorry. Can you please keep on reading the list?"

The item he hadn't read was embarrassing. It revealed something no one knew about him, and he wasn't sure he wanted anyone to know about it yet. What would Melanie think about him when she found out? If he read it, she might not like him anymore. She might think he was a loser. Then again, if he were going to be dead in two weeks, maybe it would be better if somebody knew.

"Okay," he said, "just please, don't laugh. I mean it this time."

"Fair enough," she replied.

The two of them sat back down at the table.

Jay was hyper aware of the age difference between them. Melanie was only a year older, but at eighteen, she'd experienced things he hadn't.

"Have sex," he said. "I want to have sex with someone before I die."

"Hmm," Melanie said. "Have sex, that's it?"

Jay frowned. "What do you mean?"

"Sex is sex. Nothing freaky?"

"Um, no," he said, "I just… well, I want to have sex."

Blood warmed his cheeks. Great, he was blushing. When was the last time he'd blushed?

"You're a virgin?"

He couldn't speak, so he nodded.

"It's fine, love. It's all right. I'm just surprised is all."

She touched his arm. "Cute guy like you, well, guess I figured...
you know."

Of course he knew. He had a certain image to protect. They
all talked about sex, and Jay made an effort to keep up with the
conversation any way he could. Once, when he and Sean had been
talking about their first times, Jay had even made up a story about
his. What if Sean had relayed the details to Melanie?

If it were possible, he blushed deeper. He was certain Melanie
could see the blood beneath his skin, no matter how dark it was.

Jay shrugged her hand off. "Whatever. I don't want to read the
rest of it now."

"Oh, come on," Melanie said. "You know I didn't mean—"

"I know," he said. "I'm just not feeling so hot right now."

Her forehead creased. "Does your stomach hurt again?"

"No," he said.

"You going to be sick?"

"I don't know."

"I wish you would talk to me."

"What do you call this?"

Melanie crossed her arms over her chest. "You know I'm only
trying to help you, as cliché as it sounds. With Maia being sick
now, I just want you to know I'm here for you. You understand?"

He swallowed the lump in his throat. "Yeah."

"Okay, then," she said.

"Okay, then," he said.

"You've been kissed, though, haven't you?" Melanie looked at
his mouth.

"Of course," he said.

His heart thudded hard. What was she thinking?

"Good," she said.

"Good?" he asked.

"If you hadn't been," she said, "I was thinking I could do it."

Jay's head swam. It wasn't the virus.

Melanie was looking up at him through her eyelashes.

Her tongue darted out to wet her lower lip. Was she doing it on purpose? She had to be. He swallowed.

"I'm sick," he said.

"We're all sick," she said.

He didn't feel like arguing with her. She risked her life every moment she was with him, but it didn't stop her from spending time with him. Why did she keep putting herself in danger?

Without meaning to, Jay thought of Sean. His friend still had no idea of his illness. Why couldn't he tell him? Even though Melanie knew Jay was sick, she still wanted to be around him. Why didn't he think Sean would do the same?

The answer slammed into him: because Sean didn't love him. Not the same way Melanie did, anyway. Not the way Jay loved her, too.

His face burned. His ears roared. How could he have been so stupid? Of course she loved him. Why else would she risk exposure and lie to Maia for him?

"I'm sorry," he said.

"You're sorry? For what?"

"For getting you involved in this. For telling you."

"Forget. I'd rather know than find out after."

"You're amazing, Mels."

"Damn right. I'm incredible."

"Kiss me," he said.

And Melanie did.

Several minutes later, someone knocked on the door.

Jay pulled away from Melanie, startled. The only other person who would visit him in the middle of the night was Maia, and she was sleeping in his bed.

Melanie touched her mouth. "Who's that?"

"No clue." Sean was asleep. There weren't many people left in Jay's life that could stop by and visit. He was out of ideas. "I'd better go see."

"Wait." Melanie moved her hand from her mouth to Jay's arm.

"What if it's someone infected, like a criminal or something?"

"I'm infected," he said.

"I'm not worried about the virus, Jay. I'm worried about what it can make the sanest people do."

Jay went to the door and looked through the peephole.

A short, young Chinese-Irish man with dark hair and green eyes waited on the doorstep.

Sean.

Jay turned back toward the kitchen.

"Sean's here," he said.

Melanie's shoulders slumped. "So let him in. What's wrong?"

"The virus," Jay said.

"You've already exposed him."

"What about Maia? She's sick, too."

"So?"

"It's compounded. More germs mean higher risk."

Melanie frowned. "He hasn't caught it yet. Maybe he's immune."

"Like me, you mean?"

"Shut up and let him in."

Jay paused with his hand on the doorknob. He looked through the peephole again.

Sean rocked back and forth on his heels, whistling. Two summers ago, he, Jay, and Melanie had stood on the Millennium Bridge, overlooking the Thames. Melanie started to whistle, and Jay joined in. Sean wanted to, but he didn't know how. Melanie and Jay took turns pursing their lips and urging Sean to imitate them. It took almost an hour, but they somehow managed to teach Sean how to whistle.

Jay smiled.

His hand closed around the doorknob, and then he twisted it. He pulled the door open.

"Hey, Sean. What's going on?"

"You called me at three in the morning," he said. "It woke me up. I saw you called and couldn't go back to sleep afterward. You never call so late. You had me worried." Sean looked down at his feet. "You going to let me in or what?"

Jay stepped back and let his friend enter the apartment.

As soon as he walked through the door, Sean headed straight for Melanie. He kissed the top of her head. Melanie smiled, but it didn't reach her eyes. She wasn't looking at him. She wasn't looking at Jay, either.

Jay felt a pang of jealousy, followed by guilt. What the hell was wrong with him? Melanie was dating Sean. She had been for a while. What had happened in the kitchen had nothing to do with Melanie's relationship with Sean. Since Jay was dying, she pitied him. That was the only reason she'd kissed him. The truth hurt, but it also kept him from messing up his friends' relationship He couldn't imagine hurting either of them.

"So," Sean said, "what's going on?"

Jay walked into the kitchen and sat. He gestured to the chair beside him.

"I need to sit for this one?"

Jay nodded.

"Oh, boy."

Sean sat. He reached for Melanie's hand, but she wasn't paying attention. She got up from the table, went to the sink, and refilled her glass of water. When she came back, Sean put his arm around her. She tensed up but didn't move.

"It's Maia," Jay said.

"Oh, Jesus. I'm sorry."

Jay felt like he'd been stabbed. Sean looked like he was about to cry, and he wasn't that close to Maia. How would he react if he knew Jay was sick, too? Once again, Jay was reminded why he hadn't yet told Sean what was going on. What if he couldn't take it?

His eyes slid over to Melanie. "I already told Mels. Maia's been keeping it from me for a while."

Sean sucked in a breath. "How many weeks?"

Jay didn't want to say. She had more time left than he did, but it still wasn't enough.

"Just one, but… you know."

"Mary and the saints," Sean said. "How long did your parents… ?"

Melanie glared. "Don't ask."

"Sorry. Didn't mean it."

"It's fine," Jay said, though it wasn't.

As long as he and Maia were sick, nothing could be fine again.

He wanted to tell Sean they were pretending Melanie was sick, too, before Maia woke up. Sean would ask why they were lying to Maia, and then Jay would have to come clean about his own illness.

He couldn't do that to Sean.

Melanie chugged her water. "Nearly dawn now, innit? Don't you have to work?"

Jay swallowed a laugh. "I worked earlier, just for the hell of it. Nobody's there now. No point anymore."

"Homeless people get sick too," Sean said. "Didn't think about that."

There was a long, uncomfortable silence.

Samson padded into the room and brushed against Jay's chair. Jay reached down and petted him. What would happen to Samson when he was gone? Maia could take care of him, but who would he go to when the both of them were gone?

A door opened at the end of the hallway. Not long after, Maia came into the kitchen.

She rubbed her eyes. "People are trying to sleep around here."

Sean stood and looked at Maia. He studied her from head to toe and gave her a watery smile.

"Sean," Maia said.

He stood and put his arms around her. She hugged him back with some reluctance.

To Jay's surprise, Sean's shoulders shook. He was crying. Although he wasn't close to Maia, he was still sad about what was happening to her. The virus elicited grief from almost everyone, regardless of his or her ties to the sufferer. He remembered how shocked Melanie had been when his parents died. She didn't come out of her apartment for days.

Back in the present, Maia pulled back from Sean. "Your girlfriend's brave."

Sean blinked. "Come again?"

"Melanie," said Maia, "she's handling it well. She hardly looks sick."

"Oh, Jesus," Sean said. "Melanie?"

The blood drained out of Jay's face.

Chapter Five

C'EST LA VIE

Sean turned on Melanie. "What the hell is going on?"

"She's not sick," Jay said.

"Shut up," Sean said. "Maia said—"

"I know," Jay replied. "But it's not Melanie."

Maia blinked. "What are you talking about?"

The room spun. Jay was going to puke again.

He didn't want to puke after getting to kiss Melanie.

It felt profane.

He took a few breaths and willed his stomach to calm down.

"Melanie isn't the one who's sick, Maia."

She stared at him, uncomprehending. "Who is?"

Jay's hand shook as he raised it to cover a cough. He couldn't meet his sister's eyes. When he lowered his hand from his mouth, blood coated his palm. He wiped it on his pants.

Maia deflated. "Oh, Jesus… it's you."

"No," Sean said.

His hands balled into fists. "You can't be sick. There's no way. You're immune to it."

"He's not," Melanie said. "We all thought he was, but…"

"Wait a minute, you knew?" Sean's expression changed from concern to fury. "How the hell did you know?"

"I told her," Jay said.

"You told her?"

"I'm sorry. I wanted to tell you, I just—"

"Bugger off. I can't believe you."

Sean paced around the kitchen, muttering obscenities. His pale face flushed crimson. "Why the hell didn't you tell me?"

"I was afraid," Jay said.

"Of what?" Sean asked.

"Of losing you." He paused. "Of losing you all."

"Oh, Jay," Maia said.

She slumped into a chair and buried her face in her hands. If she was crying, Jay couldn't tell. She made no noise.

Melanie was quiet, too. She sat still, staring down at her hands folded in her lap. She couldn't look at anyone. Maybe she was afraid she'd cry.

What was she thinking?

Sean spun on his heel. "How long have you known?"

"It doesn't matter," Jay said.

"Tell me."

"Three weeks."

Sean swore and kicked the counter.

Jay wanted to say something to make everyone feel better, but there was nothing to say. Nothing he said could fix the situation.

He was sick. He had been sick. He was going to be sick—until the day he wasn't.

Then, he would be dead.

"We have to find someone," Melanie said.

It was the first time she'd spoken in several minutes. All eyes were on her.

She swallowed and continued. "A doctor or a scientist. There's got to be someone somewhere who can help."

"I've looked," Jay repeated. "There's not a single human being in London who can help me."

"You might not be looking in the right places," she said. "Sean and I have lived here for longer than you have. We know the city like the backs of our hands."

"We have to try," Sean added. "We can't just let you... you know."

Maia raised her head. "I heard there were scientists squatting

35

on the South Bank. Somewhere underground, maybe. Might be worth a shot."

Jay sighed. "I've been there. Nothing underground but rats and abandoned Tube lines. It's empty."

"What about Ireland?" Melanie asked. "I've got family in Dublin. There might be someone there who—"

"We've talked about this, Mels. Our visas have expired."

Maia nodded. "There didn't seem to be any point in renewing them right away. We let them run out when the virus started spreading. Ireland's cleaner. There's no way they'd let us in, especially without papers."

"Shite," Melanie said. "we can't just sit around and wait for you or Maia to drop dead. Back me up on this one, Sean."

"Of course," Sean said. "There's got to be another way."

Jay thought for a few minutes. He'd turned over every possibility he could think of in his mind already, but he turned them over again.

Maybe there was someone in a museum who could help them. Maybe someone in a hospital. Maybe some religious group somewhere had found a cure, and they were hoarding it somewhere, saving it for the believers.

Sean and Melanie were right. There had to be a way of stopping the virus. He refused to consider the alternative—not for his sake, but for Maia's. He loved her too much to condemn her to death.

Samson rubbed against his legs.

The idea radiated up from his shins. Samson.

Some group had taken over Parliament as a base for scientific research. Samson had gotten out once, and Jay had been afraid of some scientist taking him and experimenting on him. Of course, since there hadn't been word of a cure yet, Jay had forgotten about the scientists. Besides, the streets near Parliament were closed and littered with trash. Forgotten. But he had remembered.

"Parliament," Jay said.

The other three looked as him as though he'd lost his mind.

"Parliament," he said again. "Do you remember on the news? With the woman… and the hair?" He gestured around his face to illustrate the woman's curly hair. "She was a scientist. Said they were taking over Parliament as a headquarters. They were… working on finding a cure."

"Jay," Maia said.

"No way they're still there." Sean chewed his thumbnail. "That part of the city's completely run down."

"We have to try," Jay said. "I'm sure as hell not staying here."

He walked over to the window and peered out over the city. Fingers of golden light etched through the pink clouds. Dawn. Soon, the city would awaken—what remained of it, anyway. How many people had died during the night? How many had woken up sick, like him, praying for a cure?

"We have to try," he repeated.

Maia bit her lip. Lines of worry marred her face, circling her eyes. Dark circles. Hadn't she been sleeping? Was it just the virus making her look haggard?

Did he look haggard, too?

"Jay," Sean said again.

Jay turned over his shoulder.

Sean was standing right in front of him. He held his hand out to Jay, fist closed.

"What?" Jay asked.

"Hold out your hand," Sean said.

Jay stretched out his palm and cupped it under Sean's fist. Sean opened his fingers and dropped what he'd been holding.

He studied it. His mother's necklace.

"Where the hell did you get this?"

"She gave it to me before she died," Sean said. "Part of a promise."

Jay's hand trembled. He curled his hand around the necklace. The heart-shaped charm bit his flesh. "What was the promise?"

Sean closed his eyes. "She asked me to protect you, no matter what happened. She begged me to do everything in my power to keep you from getting sick, or worse..." His eyes flew open. "I can't keep the promise. I want you to have the necklace."

Jay's blood simmered beneath his skin. "What the hell does that mean; you can't keep your promise?"

"Look," Sean said, "even if we somehow manage to find a scientist in Parliament, the chances of anyone actually having a cure..."

Silence swallowed the kitchen.

Maia coughed into her hands. When she stopped, she wiped them on the table and smeared blood across the surface.

"God," she said, "what a mess."

No one spoke for a long time. Maia made no move to clean the blood off the table.

Jay's hand tightened around the pendant. He pulled his arm back and threw the necklace as hard as he could. It hit the wall on the other side of the kitchen and rattled against the tile.

Jay slid down the wall and sat on the tile. He buried his face in his hands and cried.

"They're demolishing Parliament tomorrow," Sean murmured. "I didn't want to be the one to tell you. There's no one there. No cure. I don't know what to do."

"No," Melanie said. That was it; just *no*.

"We should go," Sean said. "You and Maia need to sleep."

"You need to sleep, too," Jay said.

"How the hell am I supposed to sleep knowing you're sick?"

"*C'est la vie*," Jay said.

Sean's face lit up. "French."

"Right," Jay said.

"French," Sean said. "France. Calais."

"What the hell are you talking about?"

Melanie stood, clutching the back of the chair. "That scientist in France, Dr. Devereaux. She was looking for patients for clinical trials." Her expression mirrored Sean's. "Don't you get it, Jay?

There might be help for you in France."

For the first time in a long time, Maia spoke.

"I thought she got shut down."

"No," Sean said. "She backed down or something. I think the French government decided to leave her alone." He pinched the bridge of his nose. "It's worth a shot."

"One problem," Melanie said. "How are we going to get to Calais?"

"Kent," Sean said. "The Chunnel."

"It's been off."

"I know."

"So what?"

"So it doesn't matter. We can drive to Kent, bust in, and take the Chunnel to Calais."

Melanie shook her head. "Don't you understand? The trains aren't running."

"We can walk," Jay said.

Sean hesitated. "Unless you're not feeling up to it."

"It might be mine and Maia's best chance," Jay replied. "We have to try."

Maia coughed again. She ran from the kitchen to the bathroom in Jay's bedroom.

A few seconds later, she was retching. Jay felt a pang of sympathy mixed with guilt. Maia hadn't told him how she'd contracted the virus. Maybe he'd gotten her sick. Like Sean, she'd hung around without knowing how she was endangering herself. Maybe if he'd come out with news of his illness, she would've stayed away from him. Maybe she wouldn't have gotten sick.

"You're right," Melanie said.

She was speaking to Sean, but her eyes watched the end of the hallway. She was as worried about Maia as she was about Jay.

He had become the reason everyone in his life was upset. It was something he had a hard time fathoming, let alone acknowledging as reality. The truth was almost too much to bear.

It had been difficult to watch his parents waste away. His father had gone first, followed by his mother. Women with the virus took longer to die for some reason. She looked as beautiful as she always had, even lying in bed on that last day, smelling of blood and sweat and vomit.

Before the virus, Jay had had a hard time with bodily fluids. Once they were the norm, he didn't even flinch.

When his mother's eyelids fluttered and she murmured in delirium, Jay kissed her clammy forehead. Seconds later, she was gone. He never regretted kissing her.

Grief tightened his gut. It coupled with nausea. He pulled a hand across his face.

"What's wrong?" Melanie asked.

"What's right?" he retorted.

"Do you need to throw up or something?" Sean asked.

Jay needed so many things. He needed Maia to be well. He needed a cure for both of them. He needed the world to somehow start making sense again.

Above everything, he needed someone to tell him why these terrible things were happening. It didn't make any sense. He didn't deserve it. Nobody did.

Jay went over to the sink, leaned over the stainless steel basin, and vomited. There was blood in it again, dark and ominous. It mocked him.

Melanie came over and rubbed his back. Tears fell down his face. They had little to do with puking.

Chapter Six
SOMETHING HONEST

For an hour, Jay tossed and turned on the couch, dozing on and off. Eventually, he got up, went into his bedroom, and started packing. In his bed, Maia snored. He eased open the closet doors, trying not to wake her. She needed to rest. If they were going to walk the length of the Chunnel, she had to get her strength up. Both of them did.

If he'd been able to stop the gears in his mind from turning, he would've attempted to go back to sleep. Even if he could only get another hour, he knew he'd feel better.

His duffel bag was sitting on the top shelf of the closet. As he set it on the floor, he realized he had no idea what to pack for their adventure. What was Calais like? How did people dress there? How long would they be gone? Did he have any clothes without bloodstains on them?

Maia stirred, turning over to face him. She opened her eyes. "What are you doing?"

"Packing," he said.

He grabbed a pair of shoes and wedged them in the bottom of the bag.

Maia watched him. "You should be sleeping."

"So should you." He grabbed a pair of socks and stuck them in his shoes.

Maia sat up in bed. She yawned. "I don't want to."

"Maia," he said, "we both know your body needs rest."

"Not that," she said. "I don't want to go to France."

Jay pulled a shirt from its hanger. "You don't know what you're saying."

"I know exactly what I'm saying. I don't think you understand." She swung her legs to the side of the bed and pressed her feet into the carpet. She scrunched her nose up as though she smelled something unpleasant. "I know you don't want to talk about it, Jay. You don't even want to think about it."

"I don't have a choice."

"Anyway," she said, "if I'm going to die, I just—"

"You're not going to die, Maia."

"Come on. I'm not stupid." She lay down on her back, staring up at the ceiling with her feet on the floor. "Everyone dies. Mom and Dad died. So will we."

"I'm not dying," Jay said.

Hollow words. He had a lower chance of surviving than Maia did, and both of them knew it. Even if they didn't talk about it, the truth wasn't going anywhere. When their parents were dying, he and Maia hadn't talked about it. By speaking out loud, it was like they made the virus a reality. They knew it was there, but acknowledging it made everything worse somehow.

"I don't want to die in a foreign country," she said.

"Too bad. We're from Chicago."

"You know what I mean."

He did, because he felt the same. Their parents had gotten sick while visiting them in London. They died an ocean away from their home.

When Jay got sick, he vowed to spend his final days in London.

Everything was changing, and it was changing fast. In a world that hated standing still, how could he stay grounded?

Jay cleared his throat. "We're going to Calais whether you want to or not. I'm not going to stand by and watch you waste away. I'll do everything it takes—"

"You've been sick for two weeks longer than I have. Doesn't the thought of traveling exhaust you?"

"The thought of dying in a world where a cure might exist exhausts me more," he said.

42

Maia got up from the bed. She walked over to the closet and started rifling through Jay's clothes. She grabbed a pair of pants and held them up to the light.

Jay knew she was looking for bloodstains, too. He looked her up and down. There was blood on the front of her shirt. None on her pants, but it was only a matter of time before she ended up like him, struggling to pick out clothes that didn't scream infected.

"If we hadn't moved out here," Maia said, "do you think Mom and Dad would still be alive?"

It was something Jay had considered, but never spoken aloud. Maia's casual tone struck a nerve. Didn't they have enough bad things to think about?

Why bring guilt into the picture—a guilt he'd tried so hard to bury?

"What do you expect me to say?" he asked.

"Something honest," she said. "The lying game has got to stop."

"When have I ever lied to you?"

She scoffed at him. "You're joking."

"I didn't tell you I was sick because I was protecting you."

"I never asked you to. Who said I need protecting?"

Bile crept up the back of Jay's throat. "Okay, just calm down."

"Don't tell me to calm down. Don't you ever."

"Sorry."

"I don't need protecting, Jay. I'm the older sister." She blinked hard against a tide of tears. "I should be the one protecting you."

"Sometimes it's not about who's older," he said.

"Oh no?" she asked. "What's it about?"

Jay teetered on the edge of a cliff. He took the pants from her and folded them. "Forget it. I didn't mean anything."

"Like hell you didn't."

"Maia, please. Can we just—"

"No." She snatched the pants from him and draped them over her arm. "You know what? I'm not doing this anymore. The lying, hiding, sneaking, avoiding thing—it has to stop. It stops right here, right now, in this room. I'm so tired of it, Jay. Can't you give me a straight answer for once, regardless of whether you think it might upset me?"

Jay took a step back. "Please don't ask me again."

"I want an answer."

"An answer to what?"

"If I'm older," Maia said, "what makes you think you have the right to protect me?"

"I don't want to do this."

"I don't care. You are."

He sucked in a breath. "You want to know why I think you need protecting?"

She stared at him, saying nothing.

"Because I'm stronger than you are," he said.

Maia's face hardened. She lowered her arm and let the pants slip from her elbow and onto the floor.

Jay couldn't look her in the eye.

In his peripheral vision, she turned away from him and headed out of the room.

"Maia," he said.

She didn't come back.

Jay found Maia on the street outside the building. She stood shivering in the morning air, arms wrapped around herself to keep out the cold. Vapor floated from her mouth as she exhaled.

Beside the curb in front of her, there was a vacant black taxi. Melanie leaned against the door, while Sean poked around inside the car.

"Maia," Jay said.

She refused to look at him. "Sean says he knows how to hot-wire this thing. We don't need the keys."

"You're stealing?" Jay asked.

Stupid. Of course Sean was stealing. They needed a car to drive to the Chunnel in Kent to maybe find a cure for Jay

44

and Maia. Stealing wasn't the only crime Sean was willing to commit for them.

Melanie's eyes met Jay's for a second. Before she looked away, his intestines jumped. Things had changed between them. If she couldn't look him in the eye, she must have felt it, too. Was she going to be awkward around him from then on?

If he closed his eyes, he knew he could still feel her lips on his. He'd have to make an effort to keep his eyes open.

Sean leaned out of the car and wiped his forehead with the back of his hand. His face was slick with sweat. "It usually doesn't take me half so long to do this."

Jay raised an eyebrow. "You've done this before?"

Sean seemed nothing but straight-laced. What didn't Jay know?

"I haven't always been the upstanding man you see," Sean said.

"Fell for the bad boy," Melanie said.

"But if I hadn't reformed, she might be stepping out on me." He winked at Jay.

Melanie frowned.

Jay chuckled and hoped he sounded convincing. Melanie still wasn't looking at him. He didn't know how much longer he'd be able to look at Sean. It had only been one kiss. Melanie had gone along with it. Why did he feel so guilty?

Jay swallowed. "You need tools or something?"

"Brought a box with me. All that's left now is to mess with the wiring." Sean touched Maia's arm. "Hey, you feeling all right?"

Maia shrugged his hand off, brushed past Jay, and plopped down on the front steps of the building. She pulled her knees to her chest and put her head down on them. Her eyes fell shut.

"She's tired," Jay said.

"It's all right," Sean replied. "She has every right to be."

No one said anything else until Melanie coughed.

Jay's head snapped up.

Sean whirled around. "What kind of cough was that?" His eyes were wide with panic.

"A normal one," she said. "No blood or anything. I'm fine."

"How are you feeling right now?" Jay asked.

"I told you, I'm fine. Tickle in my throat. That's all."

She pushed off the car and went over to sit on the steps beside Maia. She put her head on Maia's shoulder and closed her eyes, too.

"Do you have wire cutters?" Sean asked Jay.

"There are some upstairs, I think. You want to come with me?"

Sean nodded. The two of them went past the girls, back into the building, and up in the elevator. When they got off at Jay's floor, Sean stepped off the elevator and froze in the hallway. He looked pale.

"Sean," Jay said, "what's going on?"

"Jay," he said, "I'm scared."

A weight on Jay's chest choked him. The inevitability of death didn't take away its sting. Even though people were dying all around them, Jay still hadn't come to terms with the thought he might be next. On the inside, he was screaming and tearing up the floorboards.

He didn't want to die. He'd never make his peace with it. He breathed in. He breathed out.

Seeing Sean in pain—and Melanie, too, and Maia—destroyed Jay. He couldn't imagine the anguish his friends and family were dealing with.

Jay slumped against the wall and put his face in his hands.

"Jay?" Sean asked.

"I know," Jay said. "I know. Me, too."

Sean drew a shuddering breath and dissolved into sobs. It took every ounce of strength Jay had left not to follow his friend's example. He had to be strong for the people he loved.

"God, I'm sorry." Sean rubbed his eyes. His face was red. "I don't know what came over me. I think I'm good now."

The two of them went inside Jay's apartment. When Jay closed the door behind them, Samson padded over. Once again, he rubbed the front of Jay's shins.

Jay couldn't keep Samson there if they were leaving the country. He squatted down on the floor to pet the cat, mulling over his options.

"What's the matter?" Sean asked.

"I can't keep him," Jay said.

"Oh," Sean said. "You're right."

"We can't take him into the Chunnel with us."

"You're just going to let him go?"

"I have to, don't I? If I leave him here, he'll starve."

Sean dug the toe of his shoe into the carpet. "Funny how fast the world can change, innit?"

"Yeah." Jay scratched Samson behind the ears. The cat purred under his fingertips.

Before the thought of losing Samson upset him, Jay stood and went over to the closet to look for wire cutters.

The sooner they got moving, the less time he'd have to think.

Chapter Seven

JUST BREATHE

An hour and a half later, the group arrived in Folkestone, Kent.

Jay was still upset about having to leave Samson. He'd thought about the cat all the way to Kent, and he was having a hard time moving past what he'd had to do. It was for the best. It still hadn't been easy.

Nothing was going to be easy anymore.

It was funny. He'd thought getting started would help ease his anxieties. It had only made them worse.

Maia hadn't said much on the journey over. No one had. Jay wanted to ask his friends what they were thinking about, but what was the point? He knew what was on their minds. There was no need to make things worse by talking about his and Maia's situation. The less they talked about it, the more unreal it seemed.

As soon as they got to Folkestone, they headed into town to buy some supplies. As Jay had expected, the town was deserted. They passed two or three people on their way to the store, and there were no sounds of traffic or everyday life. Everything was still.

To Jay's surprise, the automatic doors in the Sainsbury's slid open as the group approached them. The electricity hadn't been cut off, which meant the store had been busy not too long ago. Looking around, it was clear they were the only ones in there. No one was at the counters. Half the shelves were cleared off, and there were containers of food and empty bottles strewn across the floor.

"Someone did a number on this place," Sean said.

Melanie let out a low whistle. "You never get used to it, do you?"

Even though they knew half the world was dead, it was strange to be confronted with the reality of it. Looters were part of any disaster, and ghost towns were as common as the setting of the sun. He hardly paid any attention to it. Still, given his and Maia's condition, the emptiness of the store—and the implication—was unsettling.

Maia kicked an empty Guinness bottle. "Wonder if there's anything in here we want."

She looked paler than she had on the ride over, and tired, even though she'd slept most of the way. For the first time, Jay noticed the bags under her eyes. She hadn't been sleeping well at all.

Had she, like him, been waking up in the middle of the night to vomit or cough up blood?

"We need to pack light," Sean said, "since we're legging it."

"How long did you say it'll take?" Melanie asked.

Sean shrugged. "I didn't. Best guess, I'd say... three hours or so."

Maia swore. "I don't know if I can handle three straight hours of walking."

"Me neither," Jay said, although he hated to admit it. He'd been sick for longer than Maia had, and he was getting weaker every day. No matter how much he wanted to, he couldn't deny his deteriorating physical state. He didn't have the stamina to walk the length of the Chunnel in one go.

"Okay," Sean said. "Fine. We can make stops."

"We're not prepared to stay the night there," Melanie said.

"One stop," Sean countered. "Does that sound all right?"

Jay licked his lips. They were cracked and dry. He was falling apart.

"I don't know," Maia said.

Jay wasn't sure, either. He hadn't walked much since getting sick.

"We can try it and see. I don't know any other way for us to get there, anyway. We have to get to France." He touched Maia's shoulder. "I think we can do it."

He didn't sound convincing, even to himself.

Still, Maia flashed them a halfhearted smile. "Yeah, you're right. We have to do this."

Melanie took out the list she'd made in the taxi. It had about twenty different items on it, ranging from toiletries to first aid supplies to food and water. "This will be faster if we all split up," she said.

"I'll go with Maia." Sean tore the list in half. "You and Jay can get the nonperishable lot."

If Melanie was fazed, she hid it well.

As she and Jay pulled away from the other members of their group, Jay broke into a sweat. Why had Sean paired the two of them together? Did he suspect something? Was he trying to catch them in the act?

Melanie nudged him. "What's going on with you?"

"What are you talking about?"

"You're shifty," she said. "Sweaty, eyes darting about—the whole bit. You feeling all right?"

In short, no, he wasn't. "Yeah, I'm all right."

"You should tell your face then."

The first item on the list was rubbing alcohol. Jay and Melanie headed toward the medical-supply aisle and found it right away. It was on the top shelf, and Melanie stood on tiptoe to reach it. Jay looked at her butt and immediately hated himself for it. He stared at the floor as they walked to get the next item. What the hell was wrong with him?

"Do you think we're going to need all this?" he asked. "I mean, you're putting together a hospital here."

"Forgive me if I'm not keen on the idea of you dying."

She dropped the alcohol into Jay's duffel bag. Something shifted in her face, and she stopped walking. "Sorry, I didn't mean to sound so…"

Her voice trailed off. She shook her head.

Jay nodded. "I know, Mels. It's fine."

"How many miles is it, do you know?"

"What?"

"The Chunnel." She grabbed a roll of bandages from the shelf. "I'm just wondering."

"I have no idea," Jay said.

They retrieved the next item on the list in silence. Jay wanted to ask Melanie what the kiss had meant, Sean was within earshot. Besides, they were just friends. Maybe she'd kissed him out of pity. He was dying, after all.

When they rounded the corner, Maia and Sean were standing at one of the registers. Sean dropped some of the food into his backpack, and Maia handed him several bottles of water.

"Get everything?" Sean asked.

"Yes," they said in unison.

Jay shifted his weight from one foot to the other. His throat burned. Before he could prepare, he launched into a coughing fit. When he doubled over, Melanie rushed to his side. Her hands settled on his back as his body spasmed.

"Jesus," Sean said.

Jay's vision went dark. He staggered backward and Melanie braced against him.

"You're all right," she said. "I'm here. Just breathe."

Sean uncapped a bottle of water and handed it to Jay. He took a sip, choked, and coughed again. His throat burned worse then. He tried to take another swig of water, and the pain abated. When he wiped his mouth with the back of his hand, his knuckles came away bloody.

"Shite," Melanie said. "You need to see someone."

"I thought that was why we were going to France."

He tried to smile, but he wasn't fooling anyone. They could tell he was in pain. He was sicker than they knew. The longer he kept that from them, the better. He couldn't stand the thought of them knowing how little time he had left.

"I'm fine," Jay said. "We better get going."

Maia watched him as they walked out of Sainsbury's. Her concern bothered him. He was concerned enough about his own wellbeing without having to worry that he was upsetting Maia. Of course, he understood where she was coming from—they were the only family each other had alive anymore.

Melanie's eyes hadn't left him, either. Her gaze burned a hole in the back of his neck. It was a small wonder he hadn't burst into flames. She'd been worried about him for longer than any of them, but she'd been hiding it.

Now that his secret was out in the open, so was her reaction.

If only he could get her alone so they could talk. It was hard to be on such uncertain terms with her. He didn't know how she felt about the kiss, and he wasn't sure how she was coping with his illness. He wanted to confront her, but they didn't have time. He would have to wait until after they found a cure or go somewhere, just the two of them, whichever happened first.

Until then, he'd have to ignore the distraction.

When they got to the Chunnel, Jay was surprised to see the entrance boarded up. The tunnel itself hadn't been used in over a year, but he thought they might have kept it open. Maybe it was too dangerous to leave a cross-country passage open. Then again, if it were only boarded, was that enough to stop people determined to get through?

It didn't stop Jay and his friends.

Sean and Jay tore the boards down in no time. Melanie and Maia sat off to the side, rearranging the supplies in everyone's bags.

Jay looked over at the girls. The sun was in Melanie's eyes, and she was squinting as she worked. A light breeze caught her reddish-brown hair and tousled it.

She was stunning.

It hurt Jay too much to think about it. He went back to the boards.

"Last one," Sean said. "Help me pry up that end. Mind the rusty nails."

"Tetanus is the least of our worries," Jay replied.

He regretted the comment the minute he said it. Sean didn't need to be reminded that Jay was dying, either.

He tried again. "Let's finish this."

Sean stepped in front of Jay and took the board on his own. He tossed it in the pile with the rest of the boards.

"Do you want to take some of those with us?" Jay asked.

"What for?" Sean said.

"Firewood. You know, for when we stop to camp."

Sean looked at the pile. "Do what you want, mate."

Jay crossed his arms. "Is this about the tetanus thing?"

"No, it's the virus." Sean passed a hand over his face and groaned. "It's driving me crazy, Jay, worrying about you. Melanie, too—she won't say anything, but yeah, I can tell."

Jay thought about his and Melanie's tense exchange at the grocery store. Of course, that was only due in part to Jay and Maia's virus. The other part was the kiss that hadn't been explained. The more he thought about it, the more Jay wondered if Melanie needed answers, too. He pushed the thought away.

"I'd better go check on Maia."

"I'll be here," Sean said.

Jay shaded his eyes against the sun and headed over to where the girls were sitting.

Melanie saw him first. She stood up and frowned at him.

Jay froze. "What's the matter?"

"Can I talk to you?" she asked.

Jay looked past her to Maia, who was pretending nothing unusual was happening. She kept rummaging through the backpack like she'd been doing all that time. Did she know what Melanie wanted to talk to him about?

"Do I have a choice?"

She rolled her eyes, grabbed his hand, and dragged him toward town. She didn't start talking until they were out of Sean and Maia's earshot.

"What the hell?" She dropped his hand and balled her fists up on her hips. "Did you tell Sean what happened?"

Jay's forehead wrinkled. "Why would you even think that?"

"I saw you two talking and then he looked furious," she said. "He scrunched his head down to his shoulders, like he does whenever we're having a row."

"Oh," Jay replied. "No, I didn't say a word."

"Good," she said.

"Good," he added.

If the kiss hadn't meant anything, why was Melanie determined to keep it a secret?

If she thought telling Sean would make him angry, then it must have meant something.

Jay licked his lips. "Why does it matter?"

"You mean you don't get it?"

He shook his head. His heart beat hard enough to bruise him. There was a tickle in the back of his throat, but he ignored it.

"The kiss in the kitchen wasn't a fluke." She turned over her shoulder to make sure no one else had heard her.

Maia was still rummaging. Sean was picking up boards.

"Yeah?" Jay asked. He was afraid to get his hopes up in case it was a joke. Melanie's pranks went too far sometimes.

"Yeah," she said. "Now let's not talk about it. We need to get going as soon as we can." She reached for his hand, stopped, and pulled away.

"Stop acting mental. Can you do that?"

The sincerity in her eyes almost crippled him. "I will."

"Fantastic," she said. "Race you back to the tunnel."

With a wink, Melanie took off running over the smooth grass. Jay watched her run with something like affection in his heart. He couldn't afford to fall in love with her, but it might have been too late.

In spite of everything he knew, he only ever wanted her.

Chapter Eight
KEEP MOVING

The first problem with the Chunnel was its lack of light. At some point, overhead lighting had illuminated the platforms. Since the electricity was off, the only light came from the dim red glow of the emergency lights. Sean tried to make a torch by lighting the end of a board on fire. Since they had no fat or oil, the flame traveled down the board and the whole thing was abandoned. They could make do with the red lights—they didn't have much choice.

The second problem with the Chunnel was the animals. Pests such as rats and insects had moved into the tunnel when the people had moved out. No one knew how they had gotten in, but they were everywhere—especially the rats, which were the biggest and the meanest rats Jay had ever seen. As someone who lived in London, he was both impressed and terrified.

It was easy enough to deal with the rats until Melanie stepped on one, crushing it under her foot. She screamed like she'd been stabbed. Jay turned around to see what happened. Melanie crouched over the rat's broken body, crying.

"I didn't mean to hurt him."

"We know you didn't, Mels. It's all right," Sean said.

"Let's bury him," she said.

"The ground is concrete. We can't exactly dig here." She drew in air and covered her mouth with her hand, bracing for a cough. Nothing happened. "Just leave it. He'll be fine."

"He's not fine. He's dead."

"You know what I mean. It's the circle of life."

"Damn it," Sean said, "can we stop talking about death?" He picked up a candy bar wrapper and draped it over the dead rat.

Jay shot Sean a look. "We need to calm down."

"Don't tell me to calm down. I can't bloody calm down."

"Sean, just take a breath."

"Just shut your damn mouth."

Jay clenched his jaw. Sean was acting out because of Jay's illness, but that didn't give him an excuse to be hateful. He looked at Melanie for confirmation Sean was out of line. She focused on the rat's still form, covered with the candy wrapper. Maia frowned.

"Sorry," Jay said. "We just need to keep moving."

"I know," Sean spat. "Every second we spend in here puts my best mate closer to death. I'm not a moron."

"Sean," Melanie said.

"No, don't you start." He whirled around to face his girlfriend, who had mascara streaks across her face. "You've known for bloody ages he was sick and never thought to tell me. You don't have a say in how I feel about this."

"We're all upset," she said.

"Sod off," Sean retorted.

"Please don't talk to her like that," said Jay. "She didn't think—"

"How I talk to my girlfriend is my own business, mate."

He hissed the last word like a curse. His face contorted in rage. He took a step toward Jay, and Jay took a step back.

"Come on, Sean," Jay said. "I didn't mean anything by it."

"Like hell you didn't." He gave Jay a short, sharp shove. "Just like you didn't mean anything by keeping the virus from me, yeah?"

"Listen," Jay said.

Sean shoved him again. The edges of his vision darkened, and the horizon tipped to one side. Jay staggered toward a wall and braced himself against it. His chest constricted, squeezing his throat. He launched into a coughing fit. Right away, he tasted blood. Darkness tempted him again. He leaned harder on the wall.

Melanie's voice was distant. "What were you thinking, you dumb git? He's sick."

"... be fine," Sean said. "I didn't mean... and he..."

His friends floated away. Jay coughed again and Maia rushed to his side and put her arms around him. His head drooped to his chest, but his brain was light.

The world buzzed around him and then, he collapsed.

It was like coming up for air from the bottom of the ocean. When Jay's eyes opened again, the first face he saw was Melanie's.

"Where am I?" he asked.

"Shh, it's all right now. We're still in the tunnel."

He tried to sit up. Her palm on his chest forced him back down.

"I'm so sorry, Jaybird. Just rest for now."

Jay groaned. His head throbbed. There was the familiar copper taste of blood in his mouth, but something was different. He'd fainted enough to know something was wrong. Every muscle in his body was slack against the floor, like they had given up their purpose. His eyelids wanted to close again. He had to fight to keep them open.

"What happened?" he asked. His tongue was thick— he struggled to get the words across it. He licked his lips and tried again. "I know I fainted, but was there something else?"

Melanie's eyes shifted to Sean as he crouched down beside her. She kept looking at him.

He shook his head. "Well... we're not sure what happened."

"You had a seizure," Melanie said.

"We think you had a seizure."

"We think, yes," Her eyes had trouble focusing on his. What was she thinking? What wasn't she telling him? "We're not sure. It was scary."

Sean wouldn't look him in the face. What was going on?

"What else happened?" Jay asked.

"You had a nosebleed." The words poured from Melanie's mouth without stopping. "Your eyes rolled back into your head, you started convulsing, you threw up, you—" She swallowed and covered her face. "Oh my God, Jay. We were terrified."

Sean still wasn't speaking. He rose to his full height and walked over to the edge of the platform. Maia sat on the bench with her legs crossed. Her head was bowed, and her lips moved as though she were speaking—no, *praying*.

What had happened to him?

"You didn't move," Sean said. "We all thought you were dead."

Jay's blood heated and cooled. He still tasted bile at the back of his throat. He'd never had a seizure before. Had his parents had seizures before they died? He couldn't remember. He had a hard time remembering what had happened between entering the tunnel and passing out, too.

Memory loss.

Panic pulled sweat from his pores and chilled it on his skin. He was falling apart. He was losing his mind. Beyond that and his health, what did he have left?

"Bring Maia over here," he said.

Maia raised her head at the mention of her name. He couldn't read her expression. She was too far away.

Sean stood and went over to where Maia was sitting. She didn't stand when he approached, and he didn't sit beside her. He stooped to speak to her instead. Jay couldn't hear what he was saying. Whatever he said was enough to convince Maia to get up and walk over to Jay. She squatted down beside him and threw her arms around his neck.

He returned the embrace, puzzled.

"Don't you ever do that again," she said. "I mean it."

"I'll try not to."

"You'd better."

When they broke apart, her eyes were red. She'd been crying. His heart sank.

What was he doing to the people he loved most? That was no way to treat anyone. Still, he couldn't tell them to forget about him. They were all too stubborn to leave him alone.

"Let's get moving again," he said.

Melanie frowned. "There's no rush, Jay. You're sick."

"I've been sick," he said.

Sean came over to rejoin the group. When he saw the looks on Maia and Melanie's faces, his expression hardened. "Wait, what's happening?"

"Jay thinks we should get moving again," Melanie said.

"We should," Jay retorted. "No point waiting around here for me to have another seizure."

Maia shot him a look to freeze lava. "That's not funny."

"She's right," Sean said. "You had us all terrified."

"All the more reason for us to keep moving," Jay replied. "The longer we sit here and wait, the worse my chances of making it out of this tunnel alive."

Maia drew her arm back as though she wanted to slap him, but she didn't follow through. When he looked at her, there was pain behind her eyes—pain and sheer horror. She didn't want to think about him dying. He felt guilty for bringing it up, but Jay was on the precipice, about to fall into oblivion. They needed to act fast if they wanted to save him.

"Please," Jay said. "We need to keep going."

Sean exchanged glances with Melanie. Maia wouldn't look at anyone, electing instead to stare down at the floor. Jay wondered if she was trying not to cry—she tended to look down when she was holding back tears.

"Are you well enough?" Sean asked.

"No," Jay said, "but if we wait until I'm well enough, I'll die here in this tunnel."

Maia shot up and slung Jay's duffel bag over her shoulder.

She set her jaw. "Let's do this."

Sean pulled Melanie to her feet before offering Jay a hand up. He struggled to rise on his own, but after a minute or so, gave up and grabbed Sean's fingers. As he staggered to stay upright, the floor of the tunnel tilted. Melanie rushed over and braced against his shoulder.

"All right, mate?"

He nodded without convincing himself. "As long as we keep moving, I'm going to be fine."

For Maia, Sean, and Melanie's sakes, he hoped he was telling the truth.

Chapter Nine

SALVATION

The four of them spent a few hours napping to get Jay's strength back up. Each time Jay woke up, he worried something bad had happened to him. He caught Melanie watching him a couple of times. Neither of them said a word about it. At one point, she reached over and grabbed his hand. He laced their fingers together.

"Try to sleep," she whispered.

He dozed but never fell fully unconscious again.

Jay was the first member of the group to get up. He stretched his arms over his head and stood. He let go of Melanie's hand before Sean saw what was going on. Thankfully, Sean was still fast asleep, and so were Melanie and Maia.

After sitting up for a few moments to gauge his health, Jay stood and stretched again. His joints popped like an old man's. If he survived the virus, he had to get in shape.

Jay walked along the platform, dragging his hand down the length of the wall. He followed the movement of his fingers, moving with his eyes down the path he had created. As he did so, a glint of light jumped out from a crack in the plaster.

Jay froze. Behind him, Sean, Melanie, and Maia were all still fast asleep. The sound of Maia's snoring echoed in the silence, punctuated by the steady drip of unseen water and the scurry of rats in the distance.

He slipped his fingers into the crack, feeling along the edges of it. His hand touched something round. He pulled away, squatting down to get a closer look at whatever he'd touched.

A little red light winked at him as he studied the lens.

A *camera*.

Was someone watching them?

Jay reared back from the wall, arms falling by his sides. He'd imagined seeing other people in the Chunnel, but never *cameras*. It was a scenario that made sense but didn't necessarily make sense, like knowing mosquitoes existed without understanding their significance in the grand scheme of things. Who could be watching the Chunnel? Besides the rats, who cared about what went on down there?

"She came down here once."

The voice was deep and ragged, jolting Jay out of his confusion. Fear dug its claws into his spine. He whirled around to face the stranger, arms up, hands curled into fists.

The man held a flashlight pointed up toward the ceiling, illuminating everything below. That was the only reason Jay had seen him. He looked like any he might have seen in London back at the homeless shelter—before the virus. He had dark skin—darker than Jay's—and bright blue eyes that startled against the color of his face and lack of light down on the platform.

"Rodney," the man said. "That's my name."

Jay nodded. "Who came down here?"

"Manners, man. Who are you?"

Jay flushed, irritated. "Jay. From London."

"Yeah? Don't sound English."

"You neither. New York?"

Rodney nodded. "Chicago?"

"Yeah," Jay said. "Grew up there."

Rodney tapped the flashlight against the meaty palm of his broad hand, making the light bounce. "She had big hair. Pretty. More light skinned than you."

A cough stirred in Jay's chest, but he kept it contained. He needed information. If Rodney was healthy, it wouldn't be good to scare him off. "Who did?"

"Keep up, kid. The woman who came down here." He gestured toward the wall. "The cameras."

So he'd seen the woman who'd put the cameras in the tunnel? "Who was she?"

"Some scientist. Said she wanted to help me, give me shelter, something to eat." He shrugged. "Looked half crazy. I told her I was fine. I can take care of myself."

Jay didn't say that, to be fair, Rodney looked half crazy himself. "Did she say why the cameras?"

"I didn't ask."

"You didn't... man." Jay shook his head. Maybe more than half crazy. "Did she say anything else? What was she wearing? Did she tell you her name?"

"Man, yeah. Said she was a doctor, like, some kind of scientist." He pointed the beam of the flashlight at Jay, hitting him in the eyes. "You an agent or something?"

Jay shielded his eyes. "What?"

"An agent. Government. World Health or some shit."

"Oh," Jay said. "No, I'm not with quarantine." He was too sick to be an agent, but he didn't want to say that. Couldn't give himself away in case Rodney panicked and attacked him. Stranger things had happened in the wake of the virus.

Rodney sniffed. "Not a cop, neither?"

Jay would have smirked at the question had he been Sean or even Melanie. But having grown up in Chicago and in a world where men who looked like him were more afraid of the police than they were of a global pandemic, he shook his head at Rodney instead.

"Good," he said. "Good. Looked too young, anyway."

Jay glanced back toward the sleeping forms of his loved ones. They had no idea they weren't alone in the Chunnel. How would they react when he introduced them to Rodney? How would Rodney react? Would he want to join them? Go with them to Calais in search of Dr. Devereaux?

Dr. Devereaux.

"Wait," Jay said. "The woman's name. Did you say—"

"Something French," Rodney said. "Don't remember—"

"Devereaux? Fleur Devereaux?"

"Yeah, man. Yeah, that's it." He scratched the side of his nose. "You know her or something?"

"Sort of," Jay said. "I'm looking for her."

Rodney's eyes narrowed. "You looking for a doctor?"

"I'm... yeah."

"Why? You sick or something?"

Wary, Jay took a step backward. "Are you?"

"Hell no. Why you think I'm in this tunnel? Had to get away from all that shit." He sucked his teeth. "Get away from me, kid. Don't you give me no germs."

Jay's gaze flitted over Rodney's body, searching for any sign he might be carrying a weapon. He stood no chance against a knife, let alone a loaded gun. He wasn't much of a fighter under the best circumstances. Now that he didn't even have his health, there was no way he'd come out on top if it came down to hand-to-hand combat. If Rodney wanted to hurt him, Sean, Melanie, or Maia, there was nothing Jay could do to stop him.

Someone coughed behind them.

Jay spun around. Maia was sitting up, peering at them through the darkness. "Jay?"

"Hello," Sean said, "you all right then?"

So they were all awake. Jay looked back at Rodney, who looked a little like he wanted to squash Jay under his boot like a cockroach.

"We've got company," Jay said.

Sean's voice was high. "Company?"

"Come over and see."

Sean stood. Jay turned around and watched him as he brushed himself off, like they'd been fast asleep on the forest floor or something. When Sean finally made it to the other end of the platform, Jay turned back to Rodney. "This is—"

But Rodney was gone.

Jay looked back at Sean. He was still there. He hadn't vanished.

"Something the matter?" Sean asked.

"There was someone here," Jay said.

Sean looked past him to the empty tunnel, the tracks stretching into eternity. He didn't say anything, but the tilt of his mouth suggested he thought his friend had lost it.

Jay frowned. Had he imagined Rodney? Had he been a fever dream?

"Why don't you lie back down, mate?"

There was movement in the background, sound, and Jay turned to confront what he expected was Rodney. Instead, Maia and Melanie were crawling out of sleep.

Sean waved at Jay. "What did you think you saw?"

Jay gulped. Rodney hadn't been a hallucination. He'd been real. He'd pointed out the cameras—but were the cameras real?

He brushed past Sean and stuck his hand in the crack in the plaster again. His fingers made contact with the lens, and when he crouched down, the familiar red light blinked out at him.

"Sean, come here. Get a load of this."

Sean hesitated. Maybe he still thought Jay was delusional or something. Melanie called out to them, and Sean waved her over. Then, he squatted next to Jay and stared into the lens. "Jesus Christ. Is that a camera?"

"Yeah," Jay said. "Guy who was just here, Rodney—he said that doctor came down here. Bet the cameras are hers."

"Well, that's a good thing, right? That means she's alive."

"Or she was," Melanie said.

Jay nodded. Why hadn't Rodney stuck around? He wanted to know what Dr. Devereaux had wanted with him. What were the cameras for? What was her reason for going down there and asking Rodney if he needed help?

The more he thought about the strange encounter, the more his head swam. When he closed his eyes, it was like they were on fire. At the same time, he was freezing—the insanity of illness. He recognized the feeling right away.

"I have a fever."

Sean looked at him like he'd grown a third arm. "Are you kidding?"

"No. I've felt better."

Melanie rushed over and put an arm around him. She pressed the back of her hand to his forehead. Her skin was cold. She frowned.

"He's burning up. We need to get help right away."

"We're in a tunnel," Sean said. "There's no help here now."

"I just need to lie down," Jay murmured. Everything was heavy. Sleeping for a little bit longer would help. Once he got some rest, he'd be good to go again. Another nap was all he needed to get better. When he woke back up, they could get moving again.

"Don't close your eyes," Maia said. She was standing in front of him with her hands on her hips. He blinked. When had she gotten up? How long had she been standing there?

"Just want to sleep," Jay mumbled. If he could just rest for a couple of minutes…

"No," Maia said. "Jay, you can't sleep. Your fever is too high, and we don't know if…" Her voice trailed off. She was worried he was going to die. They all were, of course.

He had no words to reassure them.

Jay reached out to Maia, but his hand missed her shoulder. The gesture made him stumble.

Maia rushed forward and grabbed his elbow. Her skin was cold, too. She stood on tiptoe and pressed frigid lips to his forehead.

She smelled like home. It hurt too much.

"God," she said. "We can't stay here. We have to get him through this tunnel right now."

Jay opened his mouth to speak and vomited instead. The acid stung his throat and the inside of his nose.

"I feel a little better now."

Maia clicked her tongue. "Your head is on fire. You need a doctor."

"I feel fine."

"Jay," Maia said, "can we talk for a minute?"

"Don't feel much like talking. Just want to sleep."

"I know, honey, but you can't sleep now. It's too dangerous."

"We need to start walking like right now," Sean said. "We don't have too much farther to go. If we only have to make one more stop, we should make it to Calais in close to two hours."

"Is Jay going to make it two more hours?" Melanie asked.

"He has to," said Maia.

Why was she talking like he wasn't there? Jay wanted to ask, but his tongue was too heavy. His eyelids drooped. Maia's fingers tightened on his elbow. She squeezed it, hard, until he opened his eyes again.

"Come on," she said, "let's walk and talk."

He didn't want to do either of those things. He just wanted to lie down in the tunnel and sleep. Still, he'd upset Maia. The least he could do was accommodate her.

Jay let her lead him toward what he assumed was the end of the tunnel. If he had heard and remembered correctly, he only had to stay alive for two more hours. Once they got to Calais... what would happen, exactly?

Back in London, Sean had made it sound like finding help was a done deal. The more Jay thought about it, the more he doubted anything could be that easy. Did Sean even know where the scientist lived? Was she close to the Chunnel? And what was going to happen if the virus had gotten her, too?

Were the four of them making their journey for nothing?

His stomach lurched again, but he was tired of throwing up. He forced himself to focus on the feel of Maia's hand on his arm instead. Melanie and Sean walked several feet behind them, whispering things Jay couldn't hear.

"Do you remember when we went to the lake house?" Maia asked.

"Which time?" Jay asked.

"You had just turned twelve," she said. "I was nineteen. I got to invite my friend Shante, and you were head-over-heels in love with her." Maia smiled. "You thought you were a big shot. You had this master scheme for seducing her while we were all together."

"I didn't," he said. The memory was there, but it felt foreign, as though someone had dropped it into his mind. Was that the fever's doing? The memory loss?

"You did," she said. "We went swimming one evening before it got dark. The three of us were laughing and splashing each other. We were having a great time until we realized we'd forgotten our towels."

In the Chunnel, Maia guided Jay around a fallen pipe. "I agreed to run inside and get them if you stayed in the water with Shante. I don't know what happened, but when I came back, she was treading water and laughing while you stormed out and snatched a towel out of my hand."

He remembered now—the naïve optimism of first love, the twinge of lust and nerves, and the cold slap of rejection. Jay had tried to kiss Shante, and she'd laughed in his face. He spent the rest of the trip sulking in the cabin. Everyone thought he was sick.

"She didn't want me to kiss her," he said.

"Of course not," Maia said. "You were only twelve years old."

The fever had let up enough for him to focus. Jay ran through the events of the vacation in his head, smiling when he remembered all the times Maia had come to check on him. Back then, he'd been annoyed. Now, he understood how much she cared about him—even then, when they were both bratty adolescents.

"I love you," he said.

Maia stopped walking. She tugged his arm, and he stopped, too.

"Please don't," she said.

"Why not?" he asked.

"It might be the last time."

Her voice was small, and Jay was a child again, hiding behind the curtains with Maia and giggling while their father pretended he couldn't find them.

"Say you love me, too," he said.

"Of course," she said. "You know that."

"I know," he echoed.

Jay swallowed and covered her hand with his. He was overcome by a depth of emotion unlike any he'd ever experienced. As much as he loved his friends, Maia was blood. She was *family*.

As long as she was with him, everything would be all right.

By the time they reached the end of the Chunnel and saw fingers of light stretching out through the cracks in the boards, Jay's fever had broken. He was sweat soaked and shaking. He felt like shit, but he was happy.

"We made it," Sean said.

"We made it," Jay repeated.

Sean and Melanie tore down the boards covering the exit. They fell away like paper, having warped and rotted with time and weather.

Maia was crying. Jay squeezed her hand.

"It's all going to be okay now," he said.

"Yes," she said, "it might be."

She rested her head on his shoulder, and the two of them watched as the last of the boards came down and the city of Calais spread before them like salvation.

Jay drew in the salty sea air. He knew Calais was on the ocean, but he couldn't believe how close they were. He hadn't been to the ocean in years.

Soon after meeting Sean and Melanie, he and Maia had gone with them on holiday in Brighton. The air and sea were colder than Jay had expected, but they'd had a great time. On the train ride back, Melanie had fallen asleep, her head lolling onto Jay's shoulder.

As they walked through the streets of the small port town, Jay was lightheaded. His fever was gone, but he was too weak to walk much further. He'd barely made it out of the Chunnel in one piece. Cold sweat beaded on his skin. Was he going to pass out?

Maia's hand found his shoulder. "Hey, what's the matter?"

"I don't know," he said. "How far away are we?"

Sean shrugged. "To be honest… I have no idea what we're supposed to be looking for."

Melanie shot him a look. "What?"

"I don't know where this scientist lives."

She threw up her hands. "You proposed the plan."

"What options did we have?" He stopped in the middle of the street and looked from one end of town to the other. "I don't know if we should look for a hospital or a lab or some kind of estate—"

"She's here," Jay interrupted. "That guy in the tunnel—"

"What guy?" Maia asked.

Rodney. Jay frowned. He was the only one who had actually seen Rodney. For all he knew, he was a hallucination brought on by the fever.

"I'm sure she's here, like Jay said," Sean deadpanned.

"But you don't *know* that." Melanie folded her arms over her chest. "What if we came here for nothing? What if Jay had died in the tunnel?"

"I'm not out of the woods yet," Jay said.

"Jesus," Sean said, "stop."

Jay's frown deepened. Rodney had most likely been an illusion. He shouldn't have trusted his judgment at all. He'd had a conversation with a man who wasn't real about cameras that didn't exist and a scientist who wasn't even—

No. He'd *touched* the camera. And Sean had seen it, too.

"It's not a lost cause. Sean, tell them about the cameras."

Melanie looked back at him like she pitied him, and embarrassment roiled in Jay's gut. Sean's face was blank, though wrinkled in thought.

"The lens in the tunnel. The red light." There was no mistaking the desperation in Jay's voice. "You saw it. In the crack."

Even if Rodney wasn't real and they'd never had a discussion about the person who'd installed the cameras, no one could deny that the cameras were real.

"I saw it," Sean said.

Melanie rubbed her arm. "So what if there are cameras?"

"They belong to Dr. Devereaux. Rodney said she came down here once. Talked to him. That means she's alive and somewhere around here—or was at one point, anyway."

Sean picked at something underneath his fingernails. He was only ever that fastidious when he didn't want to share what he was thinking. Melanie, meanwhile, was too busy trying to look everywhere but at Jay to offer any kind of response.

Sure, okay, they didn't believe him. But he *had* seen the cameras. They had to keep moving forward.

After a minute or two of silence, the group continued walking. Jay felt an odd mixture of fatigue and contentment. Walking the Chunnel had exhausted him. He wasn't sure if they would ever find help, or if the scientist Sean and Rodney had mentioned were the same person, let alone had a cure.

Still, he was with the people he loved most in the world. They would be with him until the end. If nothing else, he wouldn't die alone.

"Wipe that look off your face," Sean said.

"What look?" Jay asked.

"You look bloody peaceful. It's freaking me out."

"Why?" Jay asked.

"I saw that look on my sister's face, moments before she died," Sean said.

Maia swore, grabbed Jay's arm, and jerked him to her side.

"I'm not letting you out of my sight. You're not going to die right now either, you hear me? Not allowed."

Jay smirked, despite the fact that Maia looked murderous. "Since when do you get to tell me what to do?"

"I'm the big sister. Shut up and walk."

Why had he spoken to her so harshly at the apartment? What was wrong with him?

He'd said he was stronger. Why had he said that?

His face burned at the memory. He'd had no idea. Maia was much stronger than he ever imagined. How many other people could go through what she was and still be hopeful?

He hadn't given her enough credit. He owed her an apology.

Jay was about to say something to Maia when his throat seized and he lost his breath. He gasped in enough air to cough, doubling over and clutching his sides yet again.

Maia put her hands on his back while the spasms racked his body.

When he finished, there was blood on his hands and in his mouth. He almost gagged.

"First time you've coughed in a while," Maia said.

She meant it to be reassuring, but it terrified Jay. Maybe she'd forgotten their parents had stopped coughing on their deathbeds.

He hadn't.

"It's okay," he said. "I might need to sit down."

The lightheadedness had blossomed into full-fledged vertigo. If they didn't stop moving, he was going to throw up.

That was when he heard her voice, shouting from the distance.

"I came down because I heard a commotion. Does he need help?"

It was a voice Jay didn't recognize—soft and feminine, with a light French accent. She sounded at least a few years older than Melanie, intelligent and authoritative.

He looked up to see whom the voice belonged to, and his vision went dark. He blinked hard to try to clear it.

"Jay," Melanie said. "Stay with us, please."

"Our friend is sick," Sean shouted.

Jay's head was a rock he couldn't hold up much longer. A weight had settled on his chest, making it difficult to stand, let alone breathe. A pleasant tingling spread through his limbs. Was he dying? Had this happened to his parents, too?

"Maia," he said.

"I'm here," she replied. Her hands found his face. She couldn't stop touching him. "Jay, stay awake. We need you conscious, okay? Someone's coming to help."

"Who?" he asked. "Mom?"

"He's delirious," Melanie said.

Annoyance pricked Jay's consciousness. He wasn't delirious—he was dying and for some reason Maia hadn't gone to get their mother yet. What was taking her so long? Did she want him to die?

"Maia," he said, "shut up and get Mom. I need her to help me."

"Jesus," Sean said.

"Shh," Maia said. "It'll all be okay. She's coming here now."

Jay smiled. "Mom is?"

"Yes, Jay. Keep your eyes open and talk to me until she gets here, all right?"

"All right," he said.

He wasn't upset with Maia anymore. She had done what he wanted and their mom was on her way. As soon as she saw Jay, she'd be overcome with worry. Her forehead would crease, the way it always did when he was sick, and then she'd put a wet washcloth on his head. He could smell chicken soup simmering on the stove already. As much as he hated being sick, he cherished the feeling of being so loved.

His vision darkened again. He didn't fight it this time. His eyelids fell closed.

Someone's footsteps echoed off the cobblestone—they were running toward him. Maia's hands were on his back. Someone else touched his neck, feeling for a pulse.

That someone was a woman with long nails and slender fingers. Her hands were cold.

"*Merde*," she said. "We should get him inside. How long's he been sick?"

"Where's Mom?" Jay asked.

"Oh, Jay," Maia said.

And then, he remembered. His mother wasn't coming because she was dead. His father was dead, too. His sister was dying. He would die, too, if he didn't get help.

His eyelids flew open, and he stared at the most beautiful woman he'd ever seen.

"How long have you been sick?" she asked.

"Three weeks," he said. "I didn't tell anyone."

He wasn't sure why he let her know the second part. Perhaps he still felt guilty about keeping such a massive secret from his loved ones.

The woman, whose skin was a little lighter than Jay's, pushed her glasses up on her nose. She tilted her head to study him.

"Thank God you came to me. I'm Dr. Devereaux."

"You're kidding," Sean said. "We've been looking for you. We came straight from England."

Jay swallowed, and his tongue almost went down with his saliva. Rodney was right. He'd been right all along.

"England?" she asked. "How in God's name did you get here from England?"

"Chunnel," Jay said. "You had cameras in there."

"Cameras?" Maia asked.

"Delirious," Sean said.

"No, no," Dr. Devereaux said, "he's right about the cameras."

Everything was far, so far away. The horizon was dissolving. Jay didn't have time to make small talk in the street. "Need to go inside."

"Of course," Dr. Devereaux said. "I set up camp nearby in case I needed to get away. Follow me, please."

Maia eased one of Jay's arms over her shoulders, while Sean got the other. Melanie trailed behind them, not saying anything. What was she thinking? Jay couldn't imagine. She hadn't said much since they'd come out of the tunnel. Was she as scared for him as everybody else was? The thought of upsetting her tore him apart.

One minute, they were in the street. The next, they were inside.

Someone laid Jay down on a couch in some kind of apartment, but that was all he understood. How had they gotten in there? Who did it belong to? What was going on? He was too tired to ask.

His eyes fell closed again. Something heavy, cold, and wet settled on his forehead. He brushed his fingers over it and discovered a washcloth.

"Try to rest," Dr. Devereaux said. "We'll watch over you."

He wanted to ask who she was, where they were, and how she was going to help him. He wanted to ask how Melanie felt, if Maia was all right, and if Sean was still angry. A million different questions raced through his mind. He didn't have an ounce of energy to voice them.

Jay needed sleep, but his mind refused to quiet. He drifted on the edge of consciousness, catching snippets of conversation.

"I assure you, your friends are in excellent hands." The doctor's voice.

Sean spoke next. Jay couldn't make out what he was saying except for the last word. "No."

"We should," Maia said. "We might not have another choice."

"It's too risky," Melanie replied. "He... want us to... him. If he..."

Their voices sounded like they traveling through water. Was he drifting, or were they?

If he opened his eyes, would he still be in the apartment, or was he drowning in an ocean somewhere?

"No," Sean said. "Not without... consent."

He recognized that word. *Say something.* "Y-yes."

"What?" the doctor asked.

"Yes," Jay's eyes wouldn't open. He struggled to speak. "I said, I consent."

"Absolutely not," Sean said. "He doesn't even know what we're talking about."

"He consented," Maia said. "Maybe he does."

Jay had no idea what they were talking about, but he thought it might have something to do with treatment. Even if it didn't work for him, it could be a cure for Maia. With a great deal of effort, he managed to open his eyes. Maia was sitting on the floor next to the couch. He reached down and took her hand. "What do you think, sis?"

"I'm willing to try it if you are," she said.

"Excellent," Dr. Devereaux said. "We'll start testing in the morning."

A strange sense of peace overwhelmed Jay. His eyes fell closed again.

Maia let go of his hand and let it fall to the floor. He drifted into sleep.

Everything would be okay.

Chapter Ten

THE UNFAIRNESS OF IT ALL

When Jay woke up, he had no idea what was going on. Everything looked foreign. There was something damp and heavy on his forehead.

He reached up and found a washcloth. With a single touch, everything came flooding back to him: the Chunnel, Calais, Dr. Devereaux, and treatment.

He'd consented to treatment without knowing what it entailed. Was that wise? *No.*

Did it matter? *Not at all.*

He couldn't wait around for death, whether it was his or Maia's. They had to do something to find a solution.

When he tried to sit up, someone pressed a hand against his chest. He looked up to see Dr. Devereaux standing over him, frowning in the waning light. How much time had passed? How long had he been asleep? Was it sunset already?

"Where's Maia?" he asked.

"She's across the hall," she said. "We've all been waiting for you to wake up."

Jay took the washcloth off his head and set it on the floor. Dr. Devereaux made no move to pick it up. They were the only people around.

"Where are my friends?"

"Across the hall," she repeated, "in the laboratory. If you feel up to it, we'll go there now."

A laboratory. That meant chemicals, instruments, science— maybe even a cure.

He swung his legs over the side of the couch, planting his feet on the floor. Dr. Devereaux hovered over him. When he started to stand, she grabbed his arm. The contact surprised him. Her hand was cold. Familiar somehow.

"Careful," she said. "You're weak. We'll go slowly."

He didn't feel weak, but he was still groggy. When was the last time he'd had a full night's sleep? He couldn't remember. He needed to rest. Maybe if he got a few more hours' sleep, he'd feel better.

"It's okay." He lowered himself down onto the couch. "I think I'll just sleep for a little bit longer."

Dr. Devereaux didn't let go of his arm. "Jay, you've slept enough. We need to get you some food and water and check your vitals. You're malnourished, dehydrated, and gravely ill. Do you understand?"

It took too much effort to answer her. Jay put his feet up and stretched out on the couch. He turned over on his side.

"Jay," she said, *"s'il vous plaît*. Please."

He let his eyes fall closed. "I'll get up in a minute."

Why did everyone want him to use so much energy? Didn't they know how sick he was?

He needed his rest.

His legs were heavy like he'd walked halfway around the world. He'd had a seizure, for God's sake.

Why couldn't everyone just leave him alone and let him sleep for a while?

A white-hot pain exploded against his cheek. His eyes snapped open.

Dr. Devereaux stood with her hand out, massaging her palm.

His fingers probed his skin. It burned.

"You slapped me," he said.

"I'm sorry," she said. "We need to get you taken care of. Please, get up now and we'll go see your friends."

He still couldn't believe someone he hardly knew had

slapped him, let alone so hard. She was a doctor. Where had she learned to strike people like that?

"Please," she said again.

When Jay stood up, he took a good long look at her. It was the first time he'd been able to.

She was beautiful in a way that frightened him. Her lips beckoned, but her eyes opposed. They were full of a startling power.

He took a step back.

"I'm sorry," she said.

"It doesn't hurt much. I'll be fine."

"I shouldn't have slapped you. I didn't know what else to do."

She was still rubbing her hand. The slap had done more damage to her than it had to him. Maybe she wasn't used to slapping people after all.

"I'm ready," Jay said.

Without further hesitation, she took his hand and led him toward the door. The room spun, but he resisted the vertigo.

Was he ever going to feel normal again, or would every movement be a struggle until the day he died?

Dr. Devereaux opened the door and waited for him to step through it. She didn't close or lock it behind them—there was no need. No one else was in the building. Anyone who'd lived there had died already. The hallway was still—not just quiet, but still.

The hair on the nape of Jay's neck stood on end. Death oozed from the walls.

"How many people used to live here?" he asked.

"Hundreds," she said, "and they all died around the same time. The virus spreads quickly in close quarters."

"I know." He blinked. "And you didn't catch it?"

"I'm immune," she said.

"I thought I was."

She led him through the open door opposite the apartment. Someone must have lived there at some point. The furniture had been pushed against the wall to make room for laboratory equipment. A stainless-steel gurney sat in the middle of the space, skirted by machines he didn't recognize. Three massive bookcases stood against the rear wall, loaded with medicine, syringes, and every other medical necessity Jay could imagine. In the corner by the window, there was an enormous X-ray machine. He looked to the other end of the apartment. There was a treadmill with surgical scrubs and gloves draped over it. A fine layer of dust had settled over the track.

Sean sat on the floor, leaning against the gurney. Melanie sat beside him, resting her head on his shoulder. Her eyes were closed.

Maia was missing.

"Where's my sister?" he asked.

Dr. Devereaux gestured to a staircase Jay hadn't noticed. They were in a studio loft. "Up there, still resting."

"Can I see her?"

"She's your sister," Sean said.

Dr. Devereaux nodded.

Jay gripped the cool railing and took his time ascending the staircase. His body rebelled against every step. Pain knifed him in the ribs halfway up, and he doubled over, clutching his sides. It was familiar in the worst way. Last time, the pain had been followed by vomit and blood. He'd almost passed out. He didn't want any of that to happen again.

Someone came up behind him and touched his back. He turned around, still holding himself.

Dr. Devereaux stood there, frowning at him. "Maybe it's not the best idea for you to take the stairs."

He fought the urge to argue. He was in too much pain to speak.

Dr. Devereaux mistook his silence for agreement. She put her arm around him and guided him back to where Sean and Melanie were waiting. When they saw him, they stood.

Jay could tell by their faces that he didn't look right. His seizure in the Chunnel had changed everything.

They were no longer pretending everything was fine.

"I want to run some tests on you," Dr. Devereaux said. "Maia, too, when she wakes up."

"What kind of tests?" Jay asked.

The back of his throat itched, and he didn't want to talk too much for fear of aggravating it. The last thing he wanted was to cough and throw up. He wasn't going to be the one to ruin the laboratory. If Maia did, that was one thing, but he—*wait.* If he'd had to wake up, why was Maia still asleep?

"What happened to Maia while I was out, doctor?"

"What makes you think something happened?" she asked.

Sean stepped forward. Melanie followed him. She couldn't look Jay in the eyes.

"She had a seizure," Sean said.

"Worse than mine?"

"About the same," Sean said.

Jay sucked in a breath. What was he supposed to do? If he couldn't help his sister, how could he live with himself?

Melanie walked past Sean and put a hand on Jay's shoulder. "She's getting worse, Jaybird. It's happening fast. She shouldn't be so sick so soon. You've been ill longer than she has."

He knew what Sean was thinking because he was thinking the same thing—Jay should die first, not Maia. Based on everything they knew about the virus, he was due to go anywhere within the next week or two. Maia had only been sick for a week, but if she was already having seizures...

"Dr. Devereaux," Jay said, "can I please see my sister?"

She considered the idea for a minute or two before nodding. "I'll help you."

She slipped her arm around him again, and the two of them started toward the stairs. He didn't know her well, but her presence comforted him. She smelled like roses. It wasn't unpleasant.

"I hope you don't think I'm deliberately keeping anything from you," she said.

The pain in his side had let up enough for him to straighten up before they started on the stairs.

"No, I just want you to be honest with me about Maia," he said. "From here on out. Do we have a deal?"

"Of course," she said. "You have my word. I will never lie to you about your sister's condition."

"Good," Jay said.

"Good," she agreed.

Dr. Devereaux helped Jay climb the stairs to the loft. It was a slow, agonizing process. Before the virus, climbing stairs was something he'd taken for granted. How much longer would he be able to climb stairs? How much longer would Maia?

When they got to the top of the staircase, Jay paused to catch his breath. The loft was small and sparse, with a bed against one wall and a desk against the other. There was a rug on the floor, and little else in the way of decoration. The desk held a small standing mirror, a hairbrush, and a bottle of perfume.

Maia was curled up in a tight ball on the bed. The duvet had been thrown aside. She was covered in sweat and her eyes moved beneath her eyelids as she dreamed.

Jay took a step toward her, reached out his hand, and brushed his fingers over her forehead. Hot.

"Have you given her anything to bring her fever down?" he asked.

"I didn't want to give her anything while you weren't here," she said. "I wasn't sure if she had allergies, or if any of her organs were in danger."

"She's dying," he replied. "All her organs are in danger."

He sat on the bed.

Maia shifted in her sleep, but she didn't wake up.

If his post-seizure weakness had been anything to go by, she was exhausted and would sleep for several hours. Regardless of how long she'd slept before he woke up, he wouldn't be surprised if she slept through the evening and late into the night.

She'd been through a lot in the past few days.

Dr. Devereaux sat down on the bed next to Jay. She folded her hands in her lap and looked at them. "I don't know if you remembered consenting to treatment, but if you want to move forward, we need to start testing as soon as possible." She turned her head to look at Maia. Concern flashed in her eyes. "You two might have a more aggressive form of the virus. It's prone to mutation. We can't be too careful."

Mutation was how the virus had started. Jay didn't like hearing that awful word again.

His lips narrowed into a thin line. He was trying not to scream at the unfairness of it all.

Fleur's hands were soft and warm as she brushed them over his face, wiping away sweat from his fever and with it, any visible traces of his illness. Jay's pulse quickened as she touched him, though he was certain she felt nothing for him but concern. He was only a kid, after all.

"My sister was sick, too," she said.

"You have a sister?"

Her face tightened. "I did."

They were silent for several moments. Fleur knew what he was going through, then—fully understood the weight of the anxiety that settled on his shoulders. She'd dealt with it herself.

"What was her name?" he asked.

"Valerie." Her eyes lit up. "Valerie Renée. She was younger than me, not much older than you. We were best friends growing up."

"I'm sorry," he said.

"*Merci*," she said. "It's all right. *C'est la vie, non?*"

"Yeah, it sure is."

His heart hurt for her, probably more than it should have. He barely knew her. Still, he couldn't deny how beautiful she was, how good it felt to have her hands on him, soothing and cool against his heated skin. In another world, one without the virus, he might have worked up the courage to ask her on a date.

She was nothing like Melanie—that was the most startling thing about her—and instead of driving him away, he found himself captivated by the stark contrast.

"What's your blood type?" Dr. Devereaux's voice broke into his thoughts.

"I don't know," he answered.

"What do you mean?"

Jay raised and lowered his shoulders. "I'm afraid of needles. Never needed to find out."

"Afraid of needles," she repeated. "Never needed to find out."

Did she think he was one of those anti-vaccine people? Did she blame him and his family for the mutation of the virus?

"I've had shots before. I'm just afraid of needles. I mean, I even got the flu vaccine before this whole thing started." He didn't want her blaming him. He refused to hold the burden of half the world's death. "I can take them, I just don't like to. But if you need to know my blood type, let's get it over with."

"I'm just worried you've lost a lot of blood. When Maia had her seizure, there was a lot of—" She cut herself off.

Jay gaped at her. "What did you say?"

"I'm so sorry, Jay. I didn't want to worry you."

"Too late. Just tell me what happened."

Dr. Devereaux's gaze drifted down to her lap. "Maia's seizure, she... she started bleeding from her eyes."

Chapter Eleven

AN EMPTY SYRINGE

Jay sat on the edge of the bed with his face in his hands for what felt like an hour. Dr. Devereaux had abandoned rubbing his back in favor of examining Maia—something much more useful in the long run. He turned her words over in his head— *Maia's seizure, she... she started bleeding from her eyes.* He wanted to throw up, but he didn't want to move. He wasn't going to vomit in the laboratory, either.

His chest tightened. He couldn't breathe.

The more he thought about what was going on with Maia, the more he hoped he went first. That way, Dr. Devereaux could focus on saving Maia. He wasn't worth saving. He'd done some bad things. He remembered everything he'd said to Maia while their parents were dying. He cringed every time the memories touched him.

Maia's fingers brushed against his arm. The contact jolted him. "Jay, what's wrong?"

He raised his head. "You had a seizure."

"You see it?"

"No."

"Bad one?"

"Why don't you ask the doc?"

Dr. Devereaux busied herself pressing a stethoscope to Maia's chest. The longer he stared, the more he seethed. He wasn't just angry at the virus anymore. She was withholding vital information. They were in the care of the one person who might be able to save their lives, and Jay wasn't even sure that he could trust her.

"Tell me what's happening to Maia," he said.

"I don't know," she said, "but I'll do everything I can to figure it out."

"I've only been sick for a week," Maia said.

Jay had been sick for much longer, and he was only just beginning to suffer from seizures. If she was experiencing them already, the strain in her body was much more aggressive than the one in his. Not good.

"We'll need to run some blood and organ function tests. I've studied enough of this virus to know you're not in immediate danger. Still, your symptoms are escalating so quickly..." She bit her lip, lowered the stethoscope, and stuck a thermometer under Maia's tongue. "Jay, I'll need to test you, too. I'll warn you now—there are needles involved."

He swallowed. "That's a problem."

"We'll take it one thing at a time."

Maia readjusted the thermometer in her mouth. She didn't say anything, but Jay could tell by the crease in her forehead that she was worried. Judging by her eyes, she was worried about him. She was the one who'd had a grand mal seizure, and she was concerned for her brother.

A surge of affection struck Jay, so profound it almost burned. He grabbed Maia's hand and held it in his. What was he supposed to say? What could he do to ease her fears? He had so many of his own. How could he comfort her when he was a vortex of panic inside?

There was a loud clang from downstairs. Sean swore in Chinese—since when did he do *that*?

Jay and Dr. Devereaux jumped to their feet. The sudden movement made Jay dizzy. The loft tilted to one side.

Dr. Devereaux braced his shoulder. "Stay here. I'll go down there."

"Those are my friends."

"You're not well. Rest. I'll be back in a minute."

Jay took a step forward. Dr. Devereaux's grip on his shoulder stayed firm. She felt more solid than anything else.

"Please," she said. "Let me take care of this."

He sat down on the bed again and watched her walk away. Maia's hand found his again. He'd never noticed before how small it was. When they were children, her hands had been bigger than his. She used to close her fingers around his tiny fist.

When had everything become so strange and complicated?

Sean swore again, in English this time. Dr. Devereaux said something Jay couldn't hear. Why wasn't Melanie saying anything? What was she doing?

"What do you think is going on?" Maia asked.

Jay shushed her. What was everybody saying? Sean and Dr. Devereaux were talking in hushed voices. Sean's tone bordered on hysterical. Jay's stomach tied itself into a knot. Whatever was happening, it didn't sound good.

"Stay here," he said.

"Where are you going?"

"Downstairs. I want to see what's happening."

It felt like it took Jay a century to make it down the stairs. He kept a firm grip on the railing as he went, making sure to take the stairs one at a time. Every step made him dizzy. His stomach twisted with each movement, thick with dread. Whatever was happening downstairs, it wasn't anything good. The way the loft was set up, the wall along the stairs kept him from seeing anything. He had to stop halfway down to catch his breath. Why couldn't he hear Melanie's voice?

"Jay," Maia called at the top of the stairs, "come back up here. You're going to exhaust yourself."

He wanted to tell her he was already exhausted. He had been exhausted for such a long time. Besides, if something had happened to Melanie, he needed to know right away. He felt responsible—if she got sick, he'd blame himself. His mind flitted back to the memory of their kiss. Guilt seized his gut. Why had he told her to kiss him? It was a terrible idea. The virus was contagious.

Jay started down the rest of the stairs and tripped. His body jerked forward, and he tightened his grip on the railing. His arm shouted in protest as it held his weight back.

"Jay," Maia said again.

"I'm okay." Why was she still standing at the top of the stairs? Was she determined to watch him go all the way down? "Go back to bed, Maia."

After a minute, he started his descent again. It was slow going the rest of the way—his chest tightened, and he had to pause to catch his breath. His throat burned. A cough begged to rattle his lungs, but he didn't want to waste any time getting down to the laboratory.

Sean was yelling at Dr. Devereaux. She talked back to him in soothing tones, but he refused to be comforted. Whatever was happening down there was enough to put Sean in an emotional tailspin. He wasn't the most levelheaded person to begin with, but Jay could hear the serious panic in his voice. He was terrified. And now, so was Jay.

By the time he got to the bottom of the stairs, he had to stop himself from breaking off into a sprint. His body most definitely couldn't handle that exertion. It felt like he was moving in a dream as he plodded through the living room and into the kitchen.

Dr. Devereaux hunched over Melanie, who was laid out on the cold floor, flat on her back. Melanie's reddish-brown hair covered her face, which was turned toward Jay. He couldn't see her expression. Dr. Devereaux pressed a slim hand to Melanie's neck, checking for a pulse. Sean slumped against the gurney. A tray of medical instruments had been overturned—stainless steel scalpels littered the floor around Melanie. Maybe that was the source of the bang they'd heard.

He dropped to his knees beside Dr. Devereaux. His heartbeat pounded in his temples. "What happened to her?"

"She fainted," Sean said. "Don't bloody know why."

He clutched his left forearm in his right hand. Blood trickled out between his fingers. Somehow, he'd been injured—most likely by the fallen instruments.

"You're bleeding," Jay said. "He's bleeding."

"It's a cut," said Dr. Devereaux, "from a scalpel. He'll be fine."

"What about Melanie?"

"You should be resting." She smoothed Melanie's hair away from her face.

Closed eyes, parted lips. Melanie was pale, even more so than usual. Looking at her bloodless mouth, shame climbed the back of Jay's neck. If she'd gotten sick, how could he live with himself? His hormones had overridden his logic. His kiss could have killed her. Why was he so stupid?

"Jay," Sean said, "did Mels mention anything to you about being sick?"

"No. You know she would have told you first."

"Yeah, well not everyone is forthcoming about that kind of news, apparently." He shot Jay a look that oozed venom.

Jay ignored the dig. There was no visible blood on Melanie, which was a blessing, no matter how small it seemed.

Dr. Devereaux moved her hand to Melanie's forehead, muttering something in French. After a few seconds, she took her hand away and wiped it on her pants. "Clammy. Fever. I'll bet it's exhaustion."

"You sure?" Jay couldn't ignore his hunch that it was something more. The virus had come for almost everyone he loved. Why should Melanie have been the exception?

"No, but I'll confirm it. We just need to run some tests." She touched Melanie's face again, and then got up from the floor. Sean was watching her every move. She held a hand out to him. "Let me look at that arm again."

"Help me after she's sorted," he said.

Jay held Melanie's hand. She looked small and helpless on the floor, like a discarded doll. It hurt so much to look at her he had to turn away. His eyes met Sean's. "I'm sure the doctor's right. It's been a crazy few days."

Sean stared down at his arm. "Bloody well figures. I'm sick of this shite."

Dr. Devereaux rummaged through the shelves of the bookcases. Once she found what she was looking for, she pulled it out and held it up to the light—an empty syringe.

Jay sucked in a breath. His vision darkened. The needle glinted in the light and made him sick to his stomach. "I'm going to draw some blood from her. That's still the most effective way to check for the virus. Help me find a vein."

Bile burned the back of Jay's throat. He wanted to do everything he could to help Melanie, but his fear of needles paralyzed him. It was one thing to see them and another to watch one going into someone's skin. "Sean would do better."

"The hell I would," Sean said.

"You know I hate needles. I'm gonna pass out."

Sean grimaced. "All right. I can give it a shot."

"What's going on with Melanie?"

Jay's head snapped up. Maia stood at the edge of the kitchen with her hand pressed to her mouth. Like Melanie, she looked much smaller to Jay than she had before—more fragile. His jaw clenched.

"You should be resting, too," Dr. Devereaux said. "How are either of you going to recover when you won't listen to a word I say?"

The edge to the doctor's voice surprised Jay, but he didn't speak. Maia took a step forward. Her eyes widened in fear.

"She fainted," Jay said.

"We don't know why," Sean added.

"Do you think it could be… ?"

Dr. Devereaux sighed. "Less speculation and more science, please. I'm trying to get some testing done. Who's going to help me?"

"I will." Sean lowered his hand from his arm, but it was still bleeding. Red blood splattered on the floor. He swore and covered the injury again. "Maybe someone else should do it. I don't want to bleed on her."

"I'll do it," Maia said.

She and Dr. Devereaux knelt down beside Jay. Maia pulled Melanie's body onto her lap. Dr. Devereaux took out a rubber tourniquet, cotton ball, syringe, tubing, and an empty vial. Jay had to avert his eyes. He was going to throw up if he didn't think of something else.

"Look at me," Sean said. "We don't need another fainter."

Jay's stomach clenched as he waited for the process to be over.

When Dr. Devereaux had finished, she took the vial of blood over to a centrifuge on one of the bookcases. "All that's left now is to test it."

"When will we know?" Jay asked.

"An hour or so."

Maia stood and offered Jay a hand to help him up. Neither of them asked what would happen if they found out Melanie was sick. It was better to pretend that there was no way that would happen.

Chapter Twelve
STARTING OVER

In reality, it took three hours for the blood in the vial to process. Dr. Devereaux had decided the best thing to do was to put Melanie in the bed upstairs while they waited for her to wake up. "Let her sleep for a bit. Then, we'll check her again, but I'm sure she'll be all right."

Once Sean was bandaged up, he went with Melanie. The cut had bled a lot but he was lucky—it wasn't as deep as it looked. Sean didn't hate needles as much as Jay did, but he wouldn't have welcomed stitches while his girlfriend was somewhere he couldn't see her. He wasn't too keen to sit by and wait for Melanie to wake up, either, but Dr. Devereaux reassured him she would be all right after she got some rest. Sean needed rest, too. They all did.

Jay, Maia, and Dr. Devereaux stood downstairs in the laboratory proper. Maia stretched out on the gurney, fragile as a ghost in the inadequate lighting. The dark circles under her eyes were worse than Jay had thought. Her collarbone stuck out above the collar of her shirt. How much weight had she lost? How much had Jay?

He looked down at himself, frowning. The virus made him puke and sweat and bleed, and he had never given thought about it changing his appearance. What did everyone else see when they looked at him?

Was he the same Jay he'd been all along, or had the virus changed him in more ways than he knew? Was there any way of telling?

"We're going to have to take your blood samples next. I'd like to figure out your blood type in case you need a transfusion."

Dr. Devereaux pushed her glasses up on her nose. "Based on your fatigue and condition, I'd be surprised if you didn't need one already."

The thought of needles chilled Jay's blood. He'd hated needles for as long as he could remember. When he was a child, he would sit on his hands and lean back against the wall so the doctors and nurses couldn't get to his veins. He'd never had any major surgery growing up, but he had had dental work requiring Novocain. A couple of times, he came close to passing out when the dentist stuck the needle in his gum.

When their parents were sick, he and Maia had taken turns adjusting their IVs. Jay had only been able to do it because he loved them so much. Even then, he had to occupy his mind somehow, pretend he was elsewhere while he was doing it. Otherwise, there was no way he could've touched the needle.

"You're going to finish with Maia first, aren't you?" he asked.

"I've already taken some blood from her. She's AB positive."

Jay blinked. "What?"

"We need to find your type," she said. "It would be best for us to test Melanie and Sean as well. Even if your blood is compatible with Maia's, there's no point giving you some of hers when she's just as weak as you are."

She had a point, but it was still trouble to think about how quickly Maia had deteriorated. She had gone downhill faster than Jay had anticipated—a week after he'd started showing symptoms, he'd felt normal for the most part, minus a cough and the taste of blood on his tongue when he woke up in the morning. It was nothing like Maia's symptoms—vomiting and seizing and bleeding from the eyes. The more he thought about her bleeding from her eyes, the more terrified he was.

Since Dr. Devereaux's confession, they hadn't discussed Maia's seizure much.

They hadn't discussed what was going on with Melanie, either, beyond the fact she was exhausted. Dr. Devereaux hadn't checked for hunger and dehydration, had she? She'd only tested for the virus.

He turned to look at the stairs leading up to the loft. Melanie and Sean were fast asleep in the bed up there. Of course Melanie was in good hands, but he still wanted to check up on her. "How long do you think this will take?"

"Why?" Maia asked. "You got a hot date?"

Jay flushed, taken aback by her casual tone. There hadn't been much joking since they'd started on their trip.

"I'm tired," he said. "I want to sleep."

"Of course," said Dr. Devereaux. "I'll try not to keep you long. We just need to get some preliminary items out of the way so we can begin the treatment as soon as possible."

Jay raised and lowered his shoulders in a shrug. He walked over to the bookcase and studied the rows of pills, vials, and medical instruments on the shelves. As he looked closer, he saw a cage on the middle shelf. It housed two white rats, both of which were sleeping.

"Dr. Devereaux," he said.

"What is it? Something wrong?"

"These rats," Jay said, "what are they doing in the lab?"

Maia rolled her eyes. "What do you think? They're lab rats. She experiments on them."

Dr. Devereaux smirked. "More or less, yes. They're the first to go through my experimental treatments. I had five or six at one point. That was before I developed the treatment method we'll be using." She cleared her throat. "I'm sure you both realize there are some risks associated with experimental drugs. Without human trials, we have no way of anticipating how the treatments might affect you."

"You haven't tested any of this on humans?" He hadn't thought to ask the question before, and he felt foolish for assuming everything was clear. Dr. Devereaux could be a mad scientist who spent her free time cackling as she poured chemicals from one vial to another. Was she even qualified to treat the two of them? Was she even a real scientist?

Dr. Devereaux swallowed. "I have done some tests, of course. The rats have responded well."

"Do they have names?" Maia asked.

She shook her head. "I've refrained from naming them so I don't get too attached. You're welcome to name them though, if you like."

Jay studied the rats. He wasn't comforted by anything Dr. Devereaux had said. "I want to see your diplomas. Your certifications, licenses, all that stuff. The sooner the better. Where would those be?"

"That's no way to talk to someone." Maia wrapped her fingers around the cotton ball on her arm, applying pressure to stop the bleeding. With some help from Dr. Devereaux, Maia swung her legs over the side of the gurney. Then, she slid off and stood beside Jay. "The doctor's been nothing but civil toward us. Why can't you respect that?"

"It's not enough. I'm sorry." He was terrified of losing himself and Maia and everything left in the world that he loved, and he wasn't going to damn himself with any oversight. If Dr. Devereaux refused to verify her credentials, they would have to take their illness elsewhere. He'd rather risk dying on the street than strung out on sketchy drugs in a half-assed laboratory.

"Jay," Maia said.

"It's all right." Dr. Devereaux took off her rubber gloves and tossed them in a trashcan marked BIOHAZARD. "If Jay wants to see my credentials, I have no issue with that. Anything to make the two of you feel more comfortable here."

"I'm not the one who has the problem," Maia said.

Jay wanted to tell her what he was thinking, but he couldn't in front of Dr. Devereaux. He crossed his arms over his chest and tilted his head as he studied the scientist. "I want to see them, please."

"Of course," said Dr. Devereaux. "They're across the hall. Please, come with me." Then, she said to Maia, "We'll be back shortly. Try to relax."

Maia lay down on the gurney. Jay watched her for a moment before turning to follow the doctor out of the laboratory.

Dr. Devereaux led him to the door on the other side of the hallway. It was still open. Jay stepped through and waited for her just inside the foyer. He shoved his hands in his pockets. Why was he so anxious? He was getting what he'd asked for. He had every right to see her credentials—even she agreed. So why did he feel like he'd done something wrong?

To his surprise, Dr. Devereaux pushed the door shut behind them. She wiped her hands on the front of her lab coat. "Are you still intent on seeing proof of my qualifications, or have you calmed down?"

Her implication annoyed him. Yes, he had acted out of frustration, but he still wanted to know more about her. "Just show them to me, Dr. Devereaux."

"Fleur. Call me Fleur." She was at least five or six years older than he was. It was strange calling her by something other than her title. Still, they were going to be spending a lot of time together, and Fleur was easier to say. It was also easier to cry out in an emergency.

Jay swallowed. "After you."

He was nervous around her, unsettled somehow. The way she looked and smelled made him second-guess himself. He checked his reflection in a mirror as they passed and tried not to read too much into it.

Fleur dipped her head and led him down the hallway toward what he presumed was her bedroom. He felt uneasy heading that way—there was some sexual tension between them, yet unfulfilled. Why had she shut the door behind them, anyway? He couldn't push his anxiety out of his mind.

She nudged the bedroom door open and waited for Jay

to step through. This time, she did not close the door behind them. "Over the bed, on the wall."

Jay looked in the direction she indicated. There were several framed diplomas hanging above the headboard, with impressive-looking seals and scrawling calligraphy. Oxford, one read. He didn't recognize the rest, but that didn't make them any less impressive. Proof. Undeniable proof. She was who she said she was.

He took his hands out of his pockets. "I'm sorry."

"You had no way of knowing. I know you care about your sister. You only want what's best." She took a step toward him, and then held out her hand. "Do you think we could start over, get off on the right foot this time? *S'il vous plaît.*"

Jay held her hand and shook it. His skin tingled at the contact. Warmth spread up his arm and into his shoulder.

"Pleased to meet you again, doctor."

"The pleasure is entirely mine."

He didn't let go of her hand right away. When he raised his eyes to her face, the ghost of a smile graced her lips. Why had he doubted her? She was trying to help them. She wanted to find a cure for Maia as much as he did. He needed to learn to trust her, to give her the benefit of the doubt.

She squeezed his hand. He let go. His face and his eyes burned. Was he about to cry? That was ridiculous. He refused to cry in front of someone he didn't know.

Fleur stepped forward. She was close enough to reach out and touch him, which she did. She stood on tiptoe and encircled her arms around his neck.

The contact was startling, though not unpleasant. His arms encircled her waist. She smelled like roses and the furthest thing from lab chemicals. It wasn't what he'd expected. *She* wasn't what he'd expected.

"Thank you," he said.

She pulled back, slid her hands down his arms, and took his

hands in hers again. "I'm going to do everything I can to save your sister, Jay. Whatever it takes, I want her to live. Do you understand?"

Her sudden display of affection, coupled with her heartfelt dedication, sent his mind reeling. He tried to process what she was saying. All he could focus on was the way her lips moved as she spoke and the warmth of her fingers wrapped around his.

"It might be best," she said, "if we went out and got some air."

Jay looked down at their intertwined hands. This was wrong. It was all wrong. Maia was sick, maybe even dying, and he'd left her back there on the gurney. Melanie was passed out—who even knew when she'd wake up—and instead of sitting with her, he was entertaining romantic thoughts about a woman he'd just met. What was the matter with him? *Stupid teenage brain. Stupid hormones. Stupid* life.

He let go of Fleur's hands. "You have somewhere in mind?"

"I could show you around town—what's left of it, at least."

He'd been on the verge of unconscious when they'd gone through town before. Jay had no clue where they were now, not really. He had no idea what the town was like. For all he knew, Calais was another planet, another *galaxy*. *Maybe another universe.*

But maybe that meant he and Maia would live.

"Lead the way," he told her.

She smiled. "*Allons-y.*"

As Fleur led Jay out of the apartment complex and into the open air, he was surprised that the salt stung his lungs. They weren't right on the English Channel, but that was how he felt. As they walked, Jay hummed a song he hadn't heard in years, bobbing his head to the imaginary beat. He couldn't remember the name of it, but there was one summer it had been on the radio every time he turned it on.

"Diz Rocksley," Fleur said.

"That's right."

"Love that album."

He tilted his head. "Wouldn't peg you as a rock girl."

"I'm sure you wouldn't peg me for a lot of things," she said.

Jay smiled at her. The song was one he'd loved long before the virus broke all things normal. Now that so many people were dead and dying, including him, music no longer seemed to fit into his life.

"Do you ever think about how much has changed since then?"

"Since the virus came, you mean?"

"Yeah. The world's so different."

Fleur looked out toward the ocean. The white parts of the waves broke up the blue expanse of sea and sky. As they walked toward the water, Jay took the time to examine their surroundings. Calais was bigger than he'd realized, with a massive building nearby that must have been a church, surrounded by a garden that had once been beautiful, but was now overrun with weeds and high grass that hadn't been cut in God knew how long. The red and yellow flowers swayed in the breeze and made the garden look like an ocean. After a while, he got dizzy and had to look away.

When he leaned against a street lamp and braced a hand against a mailbox, Fleur stopped beside him. They sat down on a bench to rest, so close their thighs were touching. The heat of her, even through her clothes, warmed Jay in a way he hadn't anticipated.

"You two can beat this virus, Jay. You and Maia. You'll be all right. I'll run some more tests, and we can synthesize some medicine, try different things, keep up with what works—"

"Yeah, yeah," he said. "Of course we can."

But he wasn't sure of that. He wasn't sure of anything anymore. The virus had claimed so many people already and was claiming more and more each day. They were people who might have never imagined catching the virus. People who'd imagined a brighter, better future. Death had come for them all the same. It came for everyone, after all.

It was suddenly impossible for him to look at Fleur, even as she spoke to him.

"Everything will be all right. I promise you that."

His mouth twitched. "Do you?"

"Can I ask you something?"

"Me?"

"It's only fair, *non*?"

He thought for a minute. "Yeah. Okay, shoot."

"You said something about cameras."

"Cameras? When?" He had no idea what she was talking about. As far as he knew, he had no ties to cameras. "Are you sure that's what I said?"

"Right when I found you," she said. "Or right when you found me. Either way. It was before we got you inside."

"Oh." A memory, like a fuzzy object in the distance, tugged at his subconsciousness. "Did I say where they were?"

"No. Not… you didn't." At her change in tone, he studied her face. When their eyes met, the memory catapulted itself to the front of his mind.

"In the Chunnel," he said. "I saw them—I saw one of them. I didn't know what it was at first, thought my eyes were playing tricks on me. The lights hit the lens. I had to feel along the wall, put my hand in the crack in the plaster."

"Mm." She chewed her lip, saying nothing else.

"Doc—Fleur?"

"*Oui*?"

The question he'd wanted to ask since discovering the cameras—since discovering *Fleur*—reared up again, insistent and unshakable. How could he put it into words?

"You… you put those cameras in there, didn't you?"

She screwed up her face, not looking at him. "What reason would I have for putting cameras in a tunnel?"

"Dunno, but you did, didn't you?"

"*Excusez moi?*" Fleur leveled her gaze at him. "You must not be feeling well. I don't know where you'd get such an idea but—"

"Rodney told me."

"Rodney?" Something flashed in her eyes. It was something he'd never seen before, certainly not from her.

"Old black guy in the tunnel," he said. "Saw you once. Talked to you. According to him, you tried to get him to come with you."

"*Oui.* And he refused."

So, she did remember. As for his other point, she still hadn't owned up to it.

"So you did put the cameras in the tunnel?"

"I did," she said. "Not very many." The last-minute addition sounded like an excuse. Was she hiding something? No, she had no reason to hide anything. Right?

"Okay."

"It was only a few, Jay."

As though that made it better.

"Why did you lie?" he asked.

"I was afraid. I didn't know what you'd think of me."

"You should have just said so. At least tell me why you put the cameras there, all right?"

"*D'accord, bien sur.* I did it to monitor the comings and goings."

"Of who?"

"Travelers. Strangers. People like you." He frowned, and she tried again. "Sick people who need help. Other scientists."

"And Rodney."

"*Oui.* And… Rodney."

"Didn't even ask him his name, did you? Or what he was doing there? Man, I don't…" Jay shook his head. "How can you say you want to help someone if you don't even know their name?"

"I know your name, don't I?"

"That's beside the point."

"Is it?"

She reached for his hand. He jerked away, using the streetlamp to pull himself up.

"This conversation is going nowhere. I want to go back now."

She stood. "Are you ill?"

"I want to check on Melanie. And I want to see my sister."

There was a long silence between them. Jay shoved his hands in his pockets and started walking down the street. A breeze caressed his neck. If he were anyone else, in a different situation, maybe even in a different world, he might have said the day was nice. As it was, there was nothing nice about how the day was progressing.

"Jay… we don't have to go back." Somehow, she'd caught up to him. Her hand cooled the back of his arm. "I'm sorry, I shouldn't have lied to you. I should've admitted I knew what you were talking about. I just… I was afraid."

He stopped, but didn't turn around. "So you've said. But if you really did put them in there to help people, why were you afraid to tell me?"

"That wasn't the only reason."

He spun around then. "What?"

"The cameras." Her eyes were wide as she looked up at him. "I didn't only put them down there so I'd know who needed help."

"I don't know if I believe you."

"Trust me, Jay, please. I meant what I said before—I want to help you and your sister. I won't lie to you."

"Already did."

If Maia were there, she'd have told him he was being rude again. But Maia didn't know Fleur. Maybe none of them did. And as beautiful as she was, and as much as she'd helped already, there was something about her that he couldn't quite trust. She reminded him of his sister's friend, Shante—not just because he was attracted to her, but because Shante had made him think she was interested in him before shooting him down.

Could it be he didn't trust her because she was a woman?

Someone single and attractive who he might never stand a chance with?

"Let's try again, *oui*? Ask me anything, and I will answer."

Her lips parted as she watched him. It took him a minute to realize he was staring at her mouth.

"Okay," Jay replied. "One more chance. You promise you won't lie to me?"

"I promise."

"Shake on it?"

He stuck out his hand. She took it and squeezed, harder than he'd been expecting. It took her a minute to let go. The warmth of her palm lingered on his skin. Like so much of Fleur so far, her touch had hypnotized him.

Still, he tried to get back to what they'd been talking about. "Okay, then. What should I ask?"

She pursed her lips. "Whatever you like."

"You said you had a sister."

"I don't know—"

"Please, Fleur," he broke in. "You did say whatever."

Her gaze moved away from him, focusing instead on the storefront across the street. Its faded awning must have been bright green once, but now, it made Jay think of puke. Then again, what didn't?

"All right. I had a sister."

"Valerie."

"*Oui.*"

They'd gotten through that part before. Jay wasn't satisfied. He'd fully intended to get to know Fleur, and so far, she was barely budging. Had she not perhaps been capable of saving his life, or been just a touch less attractive, he wasn't sure he'd stay stuck in conversation with her if he were still healthy—and that was saying something.

"Older or younger?" he prodded.

"Younger, close to your age." There it was again—verbal

confirmation that he didn't stand a chance. Fleur was older, wiser, more mature. She'd looped him in with her dead kid sister. "She was beautiful."

"Like—" He froze. *Like you*, he thought. "Uh, she, she caught the virus?"

Idiot. Of course she had. Did anyone who died young perish any other way? When he'd lived in Chicago, there'd been plenty of gun violence, kids half his age and younger caught in the crossfire of gang warfare. But so much had changed since then. Getting shot wasn't fun, but it had to be better than spending three weeks in brutal agony while your loved ones tried not to let on how upset and scared they were.

"She did," Fleur murmured.

"How long did she—"

"Two weeks. It was quick. I left Paris when she died." Fleur crossed and uncrossed her legs at the knee, deciding instead to dig the toes of her sneakers into the concrete. It was almost as though she thought if she pushed hard enough, she could break through to the dirt below. But concrete could outlive the whole human race. "The trains were still running then—it was easy to get to Calais. Everything was easy then."

"Except losing her."

He understood. More than anything, he understood how much it hurt to watch the people you loved most in the world being murdered from the inside out—killed by an unseen nightmare. Fleur had lost her Maia. If he lost his, there was no telling how the world would end.

Fleur's gaze had dropped to her lap, and her eyelids were closed. Impulsively, Jay slipped an arm around her shoulders. She pressed against his side, resting her head on his shoulder. She was warm. Up close, she smelled even more like roses, too. He couldn't stop thinking about it. He couldn't stop thinking about *her.*

Everything was breaking down, but Fleur was there and she

was beautiful and maybe she could help them. There was nothing else left in the world to believe in, so why not believe in her? Even if she might have been at least half as broken as he was.

Fleur sniffed, breaking the silence. "Jay… when I say I will do everything I can to save your sister, I want you to believe me. I need you to believe me." She wiped her eyes. Even then, somehow, she was beautiful. "Sometimes I think I didn't try hard enough to save Valerie and it keeps me up at night. I could have done so much more for her."

"The virus comes for everyone." His jaw clenched. It was true.

"But it doesn't have to take them. There has to be a cure."

There had to be, didn't there? If not, like he'd mentioned to Melanie, what was the point in still staying alive?

"Yeah, I hope you're right."

"Either way, you trust me?"

"Either way."

He smiled a little as she lifted her chin. Instead of mirroring his smile with one of her own, she dropped her gaze again, tucking her chin against her chest. Her cheek pressed into his chest.

"I'm sorry," she said.

"For what this time?"

"For everything. I hate to see people in pain. You and your sister are severe cases… I can't remember the last time I've seen anything so advanced. All the case studies I've reviewed and the preliminary experiments—nothing comes close to what might save the two of you. I thought I had some success with my last pair of rats."

His chest tightened. "But you have two new ones now."

"I was devastated. You see, I'd even named them. It was stupid. I knew better."

"Different isn't better."

"Sometimes it is. It can be." She paused for a minute, and her tone softened. "Like you."

"What about me?"

"You're different. No one has ever looked at me as sincerely as you do. And you hang on my every word."

"Because I'm terrified."

"You listen. Because of that, you're better."

"Fleur."

She looked at him then, full in the face. Her eyes were wide as she studied him, but she didn't look nervous. Her attention drifted to his mouth, and, heart beating in his chest so loudly it was deafening, Jay surged toward her until their lips were a fraction from meeting.

They lingered in the space there long enough for Jay to understand she didn't want to close the gap.

He'd misjudged the situation. Wasn't that just perfect?

"You're sick, Jay."

He jerked back. "I didn't mean—"

"It's my fault," she said. Her fault. Like she'd been the one to lose her mind for a minute. "I shouldn't have encouraged you."

Encouraged him? No. They'd just been caught up in the moment—he'd been caught up in the moment. Stupid teenage hormones. Stupid teenage brain. The whole thing was his stupid fault. He had to figure out a way to make it up to her.

"No, no, it's fine," he said. "Just… look, can we forget it?"

She got up from the bench and dusted herself off. Her touch didn't linger on the places where they'd touched, and for that, he was grateful. Maybe she didn't hate him. "If that's really what you want."

"I don't know what I want."

For the first time in what felt like ages, he was being honest. Before he could contemplate expanding on that kind of honesty, he stood and turned away from her, leaning against the mailbox. Almost as if on cue, the virus squeezed his lungs. He coughed until he tasted blood, and then he coughed some more. It felt like forever until he could breathe again. When he finally stopped coughing, he felt Fleur still beside him.

"We should go," she said. "Your friend is going to wake up soon."

For his and everyone else's sake, he hoped that Fleur was right.

Chapter Thirteen

PROTECTION

Jay and Fleur didn't spend any time talking about what had happened during their walk. The fact they'd almost kissed had been, to Jay, a revelation. Since Melanie was the only other woman he'd ever wanted to kiss, he wasn't sure what to make of such an unexpected development. Sure, he could always blame the whole event on hormones, but hadn't there been something more to it than that? Fleur, after all, was older—and a woman—so surely she wasn't as much a victim of her biology as he was. And he hadn't imagined it—she'd leaned in, too. Even though she'd been the one to push him away in the end, there could be no denying she'd wanted to kiss him, even if she wouldn't admit it to herself.

Jay couldn't remember the last time he'd been so confused around a girl; no, a woman. Even his strange, brief encounter with Shante at the lake when he was twelve had been simpler.

Fleur was undeniably professional as she administered their treatments, ran tests, and checked their vitals. Even when it was just the two of them, she didn't bring up what had happened—what had almost happened. Jay had no idea what to think about that. He'd never been so confused, and it was all over a girl—the last thing he should've been thinking about, given his current situation. He couldn't deny his interest in her—it was far above the level of professional curiosity. If his friends or his sister noticed his strange behavior around Fleur, they sure didn't say anything. For that small kindness, he was grateful.

"Open wide," Fleur said. They were back in the laboratory for what felt like the hundredth time. He was sitting on the counter while she leaned against it. The sterile, antiseptic smell was as familiar to him as the scent of her perfume. For the longest time, he'd hated hospitals. Everything about them—from the smell of the disinfectant spray to the steady beeping of machinery and the stark-white hallways—got under his skin and rubbed against his nerves. Now that he'd become accustomed to sitting in a lab, the idea of a hospital wasn't half bad. The same scents that had sickened him once were now part of his routine. There was no escaping them.

Jay opened his mouth and stuck out his tongue. Fleur slipped the cool glass thermometer back against his teeth. It was difficult to resist the urge to bite down, shatter the casing, and fill his mouth with lethal mercury—an easier way out. He'd nearly escaped having the thermometer stuck somewhere more unpleasant, as per Fleur's suggestion. Who cared which one was more accurate? Either way, he was dying, burning from the inside out. Ebola-II had stuck its claws in him. It wasn't letting go until he gave up and it killed him.

As Fleur leaned against the counter, crossed her arms, and waited for the thermometer to process Jay's temperature, she studied him and pursed her lips. It was the second time he'd caught her doing that. A nervous tic of some sort? But why would she be nervous? He was sick, right? Just her patient. They were far from equals. That walk hadn't meant a thing.

"Tell me something," Jay said around the thermometer. Her brow scrunched. "Hmm?"

"Where did you grow up? Did you always want to be a scientist?"

He wanted to know as much about her as he could. She was a mystery that needed solving. Besides, they were required to spend so much time together—that was the nature of the treatment. It only made sense for him to ask a few personal questions.

Her looks had nothing to do with it. Well, not entirely nothing. A springy coil of hair had broken free of the confines of her headband and hung in front of her right eye. If he leaned forward just a little more, he could touch it and sweep it aside, tuck it back where it belonged—

"Verdun," she said. "Small town in the country. Nothing exciting or out of the ordinary about it. I had a quaint upbringing."

She plucked the thermometer from his mouth, fingertips brushing his lips as she did so. Jay watched, transfixed, as she studied the glass instrument. Her eyebrows knit together in concern. If he had to guess, he'd say his fever hadn't gone down in the slightest. Damn.

Fleur shook out the thermometer. "Far too high. We need to give you more medicine."

"I threw it up before."

"That was before. Jay, *s'il vous plaît*."

He shifted his weight on the counter. His right foot had fallen asleep. The medicine she'd given him before for his fever was acetaminophen, although they were both worried what it might do to his liver in the long term. When Fleur had said something to that effect, Jay responded that he wasn't all that worried for the long term, since he wouldn't be alive. If she'd been offended, it didn't show. Fleur was intelligent—she knew, perhaps better than anyone else did, that no one had developed a definite cure for Ebola-II yet. He and Maia were extreme cases, too. It was realistic, not pessimistic, to say they might not live much longer.

"I'll take it," Jay said. "Can you... bring that glass of water over?"

Fleur didn't move. She set the thermometer down on the counter, but didn't take her eyes off it. Judging by the way her jaw was working, she was chewing the inside of her cheek. Nervous? Frightened? He didn't know her well enough to tell for sure. Whatever was going on with him—and despite her medical and scientific training—Fleur wasn't happy with the treatment's early results.

"Fleur," he said again.

Whatever trance she'd been in, his voice snapped her out of it. Fleur went over, got the water, and brought it back to him. When he took the glass, his fingers brushed hers, and they both froze.

"Jay, I just want—"

"I don't want you to think—"

As soon as they realized they were both speaking at the same time, they stopped.

"You first," Jay said.

She pulled her hand back. "I was going to say... well, I just want you to know... I meant what I said before. About encouraging you."

Encouraging him? He racked his brain for a minute, accessing recent memories to figure out what she referred to—*oh.* The almost kiss. That had to be what she was talking about.

He looked into the glass of water. "*I* was going to say... I don't want you to think I'm going to try to kiss you every time we're alone together. I, uh, I've been all over the place lately, and I guess I'm kind of a disaster."

She offered him a slight smile. "You're not a disaster."

"I sure feel like one."

"Me, too," she said. "And I'm not even sick."

The glass of water was still in his hands. He hadn't done anything with it. At one point, he'd intended to drink it. But now water was the last thing on his mind. He wasn't even thirsty.

Jay set the glass on the table and leaned forward. Fleur didn't move back. If anything, there was an almost imperceptible move toward him on her part. They were so close now he could reach out and touch her face, brush the pads of his fingers over her skin— and it scared him how much he wanted to do that.

You're sick, Jay. Dying. Contagious, even.

You shouldn't be near here.

Fleur regarded him through half-lidded eyes. Her lips parted in a soft sigh. Why wasn't she saying anything? Why was she staring at him?

"You're responding well to the treatment already. Your antibody count is up. That bodes well for us."

Us. His pulse drummed in his ears, beat the inside of his rib cage. "What does that mean?"

She eased forward a half step and tilted her face toward his. Once again, he was enveloped by the scent of her perfume, the sharp yet not unpleasant tang of disinfectant.

"It means, *mon ami*, you might not be contagious."

He stopped breathing while she was still speaking. When she had finished, he started again. His chest rose and fell in short, shallow breaths that were his futile attempt at getting his heart rate back under control.

She reached toward him—at last—and trailed her long fingers down the side of his neck. Her touch left goose bumps in its wake.

"I'll save you," she murmured. "Whatever it takes."

When he leaned in and kissed her, it was better than a prayer.

For the next ten days, as Jay and Maia went through treatment, the entire group adjusted to their new normal with ease. Jay was too preoccupied with Fleur to pine after Melanie. She had gotten the message and shifted her attention back to Sean. Their relationship needed some work to repair it, but Jay had faith they'd make it. They loved each other.

Jay and Maia's treatment went according to plan. For the most part, Fleur was satisfied with their results. Between the two of them, Jay showed more progress than Maia. Fleur said that made sense since Jay had been ill for longer. She also wondered if the treatment was more effective for males than for females.

The two rats in the lab received the same treatment as Jay and Maia, but both of them were male. There was no way of predicting how the treatment would affect Maia down the road.

They would have to sit back and hope for the best.

Jay felt much more optimistic with Fleur on his side. Sneaking around with her wasn't ideal, but he didn't know how much time he had left to have fun. If the treatment failed and he died, he didn't want Melanie to be the only woman he'd kissed. At one point, he'd hoped she'd be the first person he slept with.

Now that he was with Fleur, was that hope going to change?

When Fleur first broached the topic of sex, Jay didn't see it coming. Treatment was going so well Fleur didn't think Jay was even contagious anymore—not that it mattered if she were immune.

She and Jay were making out on the bed in her apartment. Maia was asleep in the laboratory loft, and Melanie and Sean were exploring the city.

Jay was on his back, with Fleur straddling his waist, her legs on either side of him. Her hands rested on either side of his head. He held her hips as they kissed.

"Do you think," she said between kisses, "that we should talk about protection?"

Jay pressed his mouth to her jawline. "What do you mean, protection?"

"Contraception."

His head fell back against the pillows. Everything was happening so fast. He'd be lying if he said she didn't turn him on, but was he ready for sex? Maybe, maybe not. He hadn't had much time to think about it. Part of him told him it was best to wait, and the other part urged him to tear her clothes off and take her right then and there.

Jay closed his eyes. He needed a moment.

Fleur shifted her weight off of him and stretched out beside him on the bed. Her breath fanned over his neck. "I'm sorry. I just thought… well, I thought we were…"

Jay shrugged. "It makes sense."

"If you think we're moving too fast, we can take a step back."

"No," he said, "that's okay."

Blood sloshed in his eardrums. Every nerve in his body lit up when she touched him. The thought of her mouth so close to his skin made him dizzy with want. He needed to focus. He needed to figure out what he should do.

Fleur rested her chin in the crook of her elbow. "I didn't mean anything by it, Jay. We don't have to do this if you don't want to." She traced circles on the palm of his hand, which rested beside her on the bed. "We hadn't discussed what we wanted out of this… arrangement."

She made it sound like they were negotiating a business deal. It was a little more complicated.

"No, I know."

"But we can do that. Would you like to?"

He didn't have much blood in his head, but it was spinning all the same.

He hadn't wanted to die a virgin. Death wasn't imminent, but he still wanted to lose his virginity—the sooner the better. He'd always assumed it would be Melanie. He'd imagined it before, thought about it, even planned some of it. But now, a different option presented itself.

Fleur was ready and willing and single and there, only an inch away, waiting for him to make his decision—an easy decision.

"I don't know," Jay said. "Nothing's easy anymore."

She pressed her fingers against his lips. "We don't have to talk until you think you're ready. For now, it's enough that we lie here together."

Did she expect him to kiss her again? His heart wouldn't have been in it. With each minute that passed, his arousal faded.

Reality came crashing back down and forced out his thoughts about making out with Fleur.

What did it matter if he kissed her or not? He was going to die. Maia was, too. The treatment was working, but what if it stopped?

Jay sat bolt upright in bed. Sweat soaked his shirt. Too hot.

He grabbed the hem and pulled it off over his head, tossing it to the floor.

Fleur followed his example, taking her shirt off, too. Her bra was black lace, something expensive.

Jay averted his eyes. "What are you doing?"

"You took your shirt off."

"I was hot, Fleur."

She sighed again. "How am I supposed to know what you want from me, Jay? One minute, you can't keep your hands off me, and the next, you're brooding and—"

"Brooding?"

"You heard me."

He looked right at her. She was still shirtless, but the exposed skin made her look more fragile than sexy. He almost pitied her. "I think I should go."

"I wish you wouldn't," she replied.

Her face had softened, and her voice was on the verge of breaking. Why was she doing that to him? He hated it when women got emotional. How was he supposed to make them feel better?

He was powerless.

Jay leaned over the edge of the bed to retrieve both their shirts. Blood rushed into his head, filling his ears with the echo of his pulse. When he straightened up, the blood poured back out of his head. His vision darkened.

"Jay."

Cold hands on his face brought him back to the present.

Fleur was less than an inch away from him, peering into his eyes. She looked scared.

"I'm okay. I think I just got up too fast."

She stroked his cheek. "Why don't you let me get you water or something?"

"I'll be fine, Fleur. Just give me a minute."

"I could give you an iron supplement. I'm concerned about you."

"I said I'll be fine."

"Let me help you."

His tongue was heavy. He knew he needed her help, but he still wasn't sure he trusted her.

"I want to check on Maia."

Fleur lowered her hands from his face. She put her shirt back on, and then got up from the bed.

"If that's what you want," she said.

In that moment, it was. He put his shirt back on and followed Fleur out of the bedroom, down the hall, and into the kitchen. What was she doing?

As she opened the cupboard and took out a bottle of wine, Jay raised an eyebrow.

"I said I wanted to see Maia," he said. "That doesn't look anything like my sister."

"I know," she said. "I need a drink."

Jay leaned back against the counter and watched her pour the dark red liquid into two glasses. "Who's the second one for?"

She smirked and wrapped her fingers around the glasses' stems. Before he knew what she was doing, one of them was in his hands. "I thought you could use something to help you relax."

"I've not had much wine," he said.

"Come on. It's not much different than anything in London."

"I'm not old enough to drink yet."

She blinked, her eyes widening. He half expected her to drop her glass. "You've got to be eighteen."

"Seventeen," he said. "Eighteen in a week."

Fleur let out a low whistle. He could tell by the look on her face that she'd thought he was older. How old was she, anyway? He guessed twenty-one just looking at her, but she was a doctor, and schooling took time... Jay wanted a definitive answer,

117

but he'd learned it wasn't appropriate to ask a woman her age.

He stared down at the glass in his hand. "Does that change things between us?"

"No, not for me. What about you?"

He considered the idea. Since he had no clue how old she was, it didn't seem like a big deal that he was a little younger. After all, he'd always been the youngest in his group of friends.

Anyway, age was only a number. He was falling hard for her. "Not for me, either."

Fleur smiled and raised her glass. "Should we toast?"

"To what?"

"Freedom. Freedom, optimism, and the promise of tomorrow."

Those were three things Jay believed in, even though life had been so difficult lately.

He clinked his glass against Fleur's, placed it against his mouth, and took a slow sip. The wine burned his throat as it went down. Still, he liked the way it made him feel warmer inside than he had for a while.

But maybe that was more Fleur's doing than the wine's.

Fleur leaned against the counter beside Jay, linking her free arm through his. He didn't know much about her, but he was comfortable with her. She knew intimate details of his body as a result of research and testing, but he'd yet to see her naked.

She knew how to kill him if she wanted to. He didn't even know if she had a middle name.

"What's your middle name?" he asked, almost without thinking.

"Delphine," she said. "What about yours?"

"Emmanuel," he said.

"I like it."

"Me, too."

They sipped their wine in silence, mulling things over. At least, Jay was.

"I haven't thanked you yet," he said.

Fleur set her empty glass on the counter. "For what?"

"For helping me, I mean. For helping Maia, too."

He set his glass down and turned his body toward her. Her eyes were cold and beautiful. It took everything in him not to lean down and kiss her. The moment was important.

"You didn't have any idea who we were," he said, "and I was half-dead when we came here. You didn't have to help us."

"Yes, I did," she said.

"No, you didn't."

"Yes." Fleur put her hands on Jay's shoulders and stood on tiptoe. Her gaze was level with his. He would never understand how her proximity could make him so dizzy. "I did."

Rather than fight, he chose to take her word for it. He wasn't sure what had drawn her to them, but he would forever be grateful for her presence in their lives. Even if nothing romantic happened between them, there was no doubt in his mind she'd saved his life.

She was going to save Maia's life, too. Maybe someday she would even save the rest of the world.

It was easier not to put what he was feeling into words.

He put his hands on her waist and kissed her instead, hoping she knew what he meant.

Chapter Fourteen

A HUNDRED AND THREE

Fleur was examining Jay and Maia again when Sean and Melanie came back from their excursion to town. Fleur was the only one who didn't look up to greet them. She frowned down at Maia's kidney results.

Jay noticed her concern, and he avoiding talking to his friends in favor of figuring out what was going on.

"What's the matter, doctor?"

"She's going to need another blood transfusion," Fleur said.

Sean set his bag down on the floor and started taking groceries out of it and setting them on the bookcases. "What about Jay? Will he need one, too?"

Fleur shook her head. "Maia's numbers are much lower. Melanie, I hate to ask this, but... would you mind?"

Melanie took a loaf of bread out of the bag. "Of course I don't mind. Anything for Maia."

From her place on the gurney, Maia smiled. She had an IV in her arm, and her eyes looked even more sunken in the fluorescent lighting than usual.

Jay's chest tightened when he looked at her. He didn't look that bad, and they were receiving the same treatment. Why was he doing so much better than she was? Were things just getting worse for her before they could get better?

Fleur had never mentioned anything like that.

"Fantastic," Fleur said. "We can start after you've eaten. Maia, is there anything that sounds good to you?"

"Thanksgiving dinner," she said.

Jay laughed. "No can do, sis. I think there's bread and cheese and some sliced turkey somewhere."

"Close enough, I suppose." She tugged on the plastic tubing connected to her arm. "Am I going to have to keep this thing in while I eat?"

"You should. You're still dehydrated." Fleur took Maia's hand, turned it over, and studied the veins in the back of her hand. "You were worse off than I thought. You're sure you're drinking enough?"

"I thought I was," said Maia. "Every time you leave me water, I drink the whole thing."

Jay shifted his weight from one foot to the other. He needed fluids, too, but nowhere near as much as Maia. Fleur worried about his sister's kidneys—she'd told him in private. She just didn't want to say anything in front of anyone else for fear of upsetting them.

If something was wrong with Maia's kidneys, there wasn't much anyone could do. They didn't have dialysis equipment, and a full-on transplant was out of the question.

For now, Jay thought it was best to ignore the possibility something else was wrong. The virus by itself was difficult enough for them to deal with.

"I want you to drink two glasses while we're eating," Fleur said.

"You're the boss," said Maia.

Jay, Sean, Maia, Melanie, and Fleur went across the hall to the apartment to have dinner. Sean cleared and set the table while Melanie and Fleur got all the food ready. Jay and Maia sat on the couch with IVs in their arms. They weren't allowed to help—Fleur told them to focus their energy on healing.

As Melanie helped Fleur, every couple of minutes she made eye contact with Jay. They held the contact for a moment, but Melanie looked away.

She always looked away.

Did she know what was going on between Jay and Fleur?

121

His affair with the scientist had distanced him from his friends. Maybe Melanie had sensed the growing divide. Maybe she was even jealous of his relationship with Fleur. After all, Melanie had confessed her interest in him before they went into the Chunnel.

How much of that conversation did he remember? That was before the seizure and the fever that had almost killed him. The virus was affecting his memory, but he wasn't sure how much.

His parents, sweaty and delirious, had forgotten their children's faces in their final days.

Jay refused to forget the ones he loved most.

He got up from the couch and went over to the table. Fleur scowled when she saw him, but he ignored her.

"Let me help prepare the food," he said.

"You're ill," Fleur said. "You should be resting. If you want to help me, that's what you can do."

His brow furrowed. Of course, she worried about him, but the tone behind her words was too unprofessional. Did she hear it? She was going to give them away.

Jay's mouth was dry. "I've had enough of resting. I need something else to do."

Fleur shook her head, but she didn't say anything else. He wanted to ask if he could take the IV out of his arm yet—he didn't feel like he needed it—but it wasn't the best time. He would just have to deal with the minor inconvenience.

Melanie still wasn't looking at him. What was going on? Did she have an inkling of his affair with Fleur, or was there something else bothering her? Whatever it was, Jay wanted to get to the bottom of it. He wanted to find a way to get Melanie alone—maybe then she'd feel like talking to him—but how?

"You all right, mate?"

Sean was looking at him. Jay withered under his friend's scrutiny. It was wrong to even think about Melanie with Sean around.

"Fine," Jay said, "thank you." The next sentence burst out of him without hesitation. "Mels, do you think we could talk for a minute?"

Blood rushed into Melanie's pale cheeks. Without a word, she nodded. She looked scared, but still, she nodded.

Sean's face scrunched up. "Is something wrong?"

"It's nothing," Jay said.

"It was nothing before," Sean said. "Nothing might kill you."

Jay didn't like the way Sean's mouth turned down into a scowl. Before Jay's illness, they'd always trusted each other. Before the Chunnel, Jay thought Sean would get over Jay's keeping the virus a secret. After all, they had bigger things to worry about than lying by omission.

Besides, couldn't Sean understand Jay had been trying to keep him safe from the awful truth? He'd wanted to spare Sean's feelings. Regardless of the execution, that was his intention. With that in mind, couldn't Sean overlook the rest?

"Please," Jay said, to no one in particular.

"It's fine," Melanie said. "It's only a moment."

Without waiting for some sign she'd follow him, Jay turned and headed to the back of the long hallway. He heard Sean mutter something under his breath, but Jay was still within earshot.

Melanie's footfalls squished softly in the carpet. Somehow, she still trusted him.

Jay led her into the open bedroom and closed the door. His hand lingered on the doorknob. Would Sean suspect something because the door was closed? He couldn't leave it open—he might be spilling secrets.

His fingers dropped from the doorknob. He shoved his hands in his pockets.

Melanie sat down on the end of the bed. She'd been sweating— her reddish-brown hair clung to the side of her face. Still, he couldn't help staring at her. She was extraordinary.

"I promise you this won't take long," he said.

"Fine," she replied.

He wasn't sure how to get started. Every muscle in his body tensed.

"You've been... well, I feel like... um." He reached up and rubbed the back of his neck. "I feel hurt when I think there's something gone wrong between us. It seems like I'm being, uh, ignored. Lately, I mean."

Her pale eyes focused on his dark ones. "Ignored?"

"You don't look me in the eye. Like right now, I think this is the first time you've looked at me since we got here."

Her slim fingers dug into the duvet cover. She kept her eyes on his. "It hasn't been intentional."

Women were confusing. What the hell did that mean?

Jay took his hands out of his pockets and crossed them over his chest. At this rate, they'd never get things sorted out. "Is there something I've said or done to offend you?" As terrified as he was of hearing her answer, he knew it was the only way for them to move forward.

"I don't know," she said.

"You don't know?"

"No. I'm sorry."

He sat down next to her on the bed. The spring squeaked beneath him.

"What do you mean?"

"I don't know," she repeated. "I just... don't know anything anymore."

Before he could reassure her, she threw her arms around his neck and buried her face in his shoulder.

At first, he thought she was crying, but her shoulders weren't moving and she made no sound. He stroked her back, uncertain, and tried to ignore the feeling of her body against his.

It was everything he thought he wanted with Fleur, only it was no longer happening with Fleur. It had started with Melanie, and no matter how hard he fought himself, it might end with her.

He wasn't sure how much longer he could maintain his resolve.

Fighting feelings was exhausting.

"Melanie," he said.

She didn't move. She didn't say a word or give any sign she'd heard him.

"Mels," he tried again.

She mumbled something against his shirt.

"Can't understand you, Mels."

Melanie propped her chin against him and peered up at him. Her eyes were wet—she'd been crying. He'd underestimated her again.

"I know about you and Dr. Devereaux."

The sentence punched him in the gut. It was what he'd most dreaded hearing her say, but now that it was out in the open, he wasn't sure why. He'd be eighteen soon, an adult, and no one could tell him what to do—including Melanie. Even if she disapproved, what did it matter to him?

"That's what you're upset about?"

She pulled away from him. "I don't think it's best to get involved with her, Jay. Something's off about her."

The more she spoke, the more defensive he felt. She didn't know what she was talking about. She had little to do with Fleur, and she hadn't spent as much time alone with her as Jay had.

Why was she making such harsh accusations?

"What makes you say that?"

"I don't know anything for certain," Melanie said, "but she just seems… dangerous. I don't know why she's pursuing you, but I don't think—"

"You don't think I'm worth it?"

"That's not what I said."

Jay scoffed. He got up from the bed and paced the length of the bedroom.

Who the hell did she think she was? Where did she get off telling him who he could and couldn't carry on affairs with?

She knew good and well how he felt about her. She claimed

she felt the same way, yet she was still with Sean. He knew she hadn't told him how she felt about Jay.

If Melanie rejected Jay, did she expect him to come crawling back when she broke up with Sean?

Jay threw up on the carpet. He was almost as shocked as Melanie was, if not more so. He couldn't remember the last time he'd thrown up. The treatment had been working well.

"Stay here," Melanie said. "I'll get the doctor."

His whole body trembled. Should he sit down again? The room spun.

Was he going to faint, just because of vomiting? He couldn't have become that weak.

Still, he made his way over to the bed again. Better safe than sorry.

He lay down, closed his eyes, and put his hands on his stomach. His ribs were sticking out. When had he lost so much weight? He hadn't been sick that long. The virus was more aggressive than he gave it credit for.

Fleur's voice shook him from his half trance. His eyes flew open. All he saw was ceiling. Then, Fleur's face popped into sight.

"*Merde*," she said. "Shit. What happened to you?"

"I threw up," he said.

"I see."

"I'll clean it later."

"Never mind," she said. "Let me go get the thermometer."

Fleur disappeared from view again. Jay took a deep breath. His stomach was still unsettled, but he didn't think he was going to puke again. He hoped to God he wasn't going to puke in front of Fleur.

When Fleur came back, she stuck the thermometer under his tongue.

They waited in silence for the reading to appear. After a minute, the thermometer beeped. Fleur snatched it out of Jay's mouth so quickly he feared he'd swallowed it somehow—one minute, it was there; the next, simply gone.

She pushed her glasses up on the bridge of her nose.

Jay studied her face as she studied the screen.

When she spoke again, he got the sense it wasn't going to be good.

"A hundred and three, Jay. The treatment stopped working. You might have developed a tolerance to it."

Chapter Fifteen
SICK AGAIN

Jay never imagined Fleur would see him naked for the first time as she lowered his body into an ice bath.

To say the situation was less than ideal would have been an understatement.

He'd had nightmares about losing his clothes in a public place. The situation was like that, with the added bonus of having a romantic partner present.

In a way, the fever was a blessing in disguise. If he survived it, he wouldn't remember stripping in front of Fleur and collapsing in the bathtub.

His delirious thoughts ran the gamut from embarrassed to terrified. Embarrassed because he hadn't taken off his clothes for a woman before, let alone one he liked. Terrified because the fever was taking over and threatening to rip him to shreds.

Fleur flitted over him and poured ice-cold water over his head to keep him conscious. There was a sense of foreignness, like he wasn't connected to his body. He was floating above the scene, watching it unfold.

He didn't come back down until he heard the words *I love you*.

He heard them with his ears, but they settled in his stomach.

Everything was changing, and it was changing fast. He yearned to tell Fleur how he felt, to cross the rift between them, but he didn't know how.

He managed her name, and her hand brushed his cheek.

That was all he remembered.

Maia was the one who came in to wake him.

He'd been sleeping in Fleur's bed. How had he gotten from the bath to the bed? He didn't remember anything beyond Fleur pouring freezing water on him.

"Dr. Devereaux wants to increase the dosage," Maia said as she opened the blinds. Sunlight poured in through the wide windows, spreading out over the floor. Was it the same day as it had been or already the next? "She thinks your body is more responsive, which means I could see side effects soon if we don't make a change."

"You mean, you'll get sick again like I did," he said.

"We're both still sick."

"I know. But you know what I mean."

Maia chewed the inside of her cheek, the way she did whenever she had something on her mind. It had always been Jay's way of knowing when something was wrong, and he had learned to pay attention to it.

He sat up against the pillows. "What's going on?"

"I'm not sure I want to tell you."

"Now you *have* to tell me."

A muscle jerked in her jaw. "It's about Sean."

"What about him?"

"He doesn't want Melanie around you anymore."

Jay's stomach dropped into his feet. He slumped against the pillows and let his head loll back. So that was it, then—Melanie had told Sean what was going on. The timing was terrible, but then again, he knew it had to happen sometime. They couldn't have kept it a secret forever.

"I'm sorry," Maia said. "I know this must be hard."

It was so much more, but what had he expected? It wasn't as though they could run off in the middle of the night and elope. There were still people alive who would ask questions and worry if they disappeared.

"I'll be okay," Jay said.

It took Maia a minute to say anything else. "Sean doesn't want much to do with you either. I tried talking to him about it, but I don't think he'll budge."

He should have known Sean would find out sooner rather than later. He and Melanie had been running around town a great deal lately. They were bound to talk.

What had Melanie said to him? How had she explained what was happening between them?

"How does Melanie feel?" Jay asked Maia.

"She just wants to make Sean happy. She's upset, but she understands that's the only way to keep him content." Maia frowned. "I expected you to be more offended than this. I know I am."

"You are?"

"Of course. Sean makes it seem like you and I haven't been contagious this entire time."

Jay blinked. What did she mean?

"Contagious?"

"Yes," she said. "That's why he doesn't want Melanie spending any more time with you. He's afraid she'll catch the virus."

A bizarre mixture of indignance and relief broke over Jay like a wave. On the one hand, Sean presumably still had no clue what was going on with him and Melanie. Still, he wanted everyone to treat Jay like a leper.

"Jay… what did you think I was going to say?"

Maia had always been good at reading him, just as he had gotten comfortable with reading her. Should he keep lying or open up?

Maybe she wouldn't care much about the affair. Maybe she would even sympathize with him once she knew what he was going through.

He didn't have to tell her anything about Fleur, though. There was enough drama already.

Jay swallowed. He tasted blood, and he wasn't sure where it

had come from.

A guttural moan came from Maia's throat. Her eyes rolled up into her head until all he saw was white. Then, she toppled forward on the bed.

Jay leaped to his feet. His blood froze in his veins. Horrified, he watched as Maia seized on the bed. He knew he should call for help, but he couldn't move. He had never seen someone have a seizure before.

Was that what had happened to him back in the Chunnel?

Maia threw up, and the vomit had blood in it, as well as some kind of foam. Pre-virus Jay would've puked at the sight. Not many things turned his stomach anymore.

To keep his sister from choking, he managed to turn her on her side. He kept a white-knuckled grip on her shoulder. If he let go, he didn't know what would happen.

He called for the doctor. Her first name came out instead.

"Fleur!"

She rushed in faster than Jay had anticipated. Her face was flushed, her eyes wide with panic.

"What's going on? What happened?" Without waiting for an explanation, she sat down beside Maia on the bed. "Holy Mother. How long?"

"How long what?" he asked.

"What do you think? How long has she been seizing?"

He didn't know. Everything had happened so fast, and now the seconds crawled by at a glacial pace.

Jay took his hand off Maia's shoulder. "A few minutes, I guess. I didn't know what to do."

"Move," Fleur said.

She didn't have to ask twice. He got up from the bed. His legs shook so much he could barely stand on them. His pulse bruised the inside of his ribs. Wasn't there anything he could do to help Maia? There had to be some way for him to get help.

"What's wrong?" he asked.

"Another seizure."

"A bad one?"

She shot him a look. "Is there any other kind?"

"Tell me how to help, what to do."

"Get out of here, all right? Let me do my job."

Stunned as he was by the sharpness of her tone, Jay backed away. He went out of the room without another word or a second glance at Maia. He was better off not seeing her.

Melanie and Sean were sitting on the couch in the living room. They stood when Jay came into view.

"You all right?" Sean asked.

"It wasn't me."

"Maia?"

He nodded. "A seizure. Pretty bad one again."

Melanie pressed a hand to her mouth. Her skin was paler than Jay had ever seen it. In that moment, Sean didn't seem to care she was in the same room as Jay. In that moment, her catching the virus was the last thing on his mind.

Maia was in danger.

Jay went into the kitchen. He opened the refrigerator, took out a bottle of wine, grabbed a glass, and poured himself a drink.

When Melanie came after him, he was already halfway through downing the contents of the glass.

Sean wasn't around.

"What are you doing?"

"What does it look like?" He reached around her and took another glass down from the cupboard. "Would you care to join me?"

Her smile wavered. "I don't think so, thanks."

"Come on," he said. "A few sips won't kill you."

She chewed her lip, watching in silence as he poured the wine into the second glass. He handed it to her, and she took it. Her hand was trembling.

"Do you think this is going to help you?" she asked.

Jay refilled his glass and raised it to his lips. "I don't know, but I don't think it can make anything worse."

He lowered the glass, paused, and then held it toward Melanie. "I think we should toast."

"What's gotten into you?"

"To mortality," he said.

She opened her mouth, but no sound came out. Jay clinked his glass against hers and chugged the wine in one swallow. He set his empty glass back on the counter. Melanie was still holding hers, and she hadn't bothered to take a sip.

"Go on," he said.

She set the glass down on the counter. "I'm not doing this with you. It's terrible, Jay."

"What is?"

"This ridiculous front you're putting up. You're terrified, but you can't just come out and say it. You'd rather be callous." She folded her arms.

"You have no idea how much it hurts me. When you act like you don't care whether you live or die, it tears me up inside."

He put on a brave face to spare his friends. If what Melanie said were true, he was only making things worse. He was pouring salt in the open, festering wound their friendship had become. He was mocking their emotion.

Jay wanted to vomit. It wasn't the virus.

He wanted to apologize. Instead, he asked, "Where's Sean?"

"Back there with Maia and Dr. Devereaux. Jay—" She threw herself at him again, latching onto his shirt. "Don't do this to us, please. Don't do it to me."

Guilt and regret clawed their way through his chest. How could he have been so stupid? If anyone treated him the way he'd treated Sean and Melanie, he would've had a fit. He knew better than to behave the way he was—why couldn't he change? What the hell was wrong with him?

Something was holding him back from acknowledging his

feelings. He needed to figure out what. He needed to process. He needed to breathe.

"I need air," he said.

Melanie released him and took a step back. "Sorry?"

The kitchen was stifling. Sweat dripped down the back of Jay's neck and trailed between his shoulder blades. His stomach pitched around like a ship in a storm.

"You don't look well," Melanie said.

He didn't feel well, either. He needed to lie down.

"Dr. Devereaux," he said.

"She's busy helping Maia. Are you going to be sick? Do you need to drink some water?"

He needed anything and everything and nothing all at once. His brain was burning. The fever raged.

"Need," he said.

"What? What do you need?"

Need you. Need Fleur. Need my parents.

"Jay, tell me."

How could he put the whole world into words?

"I think I'm going to die," he said. "I feel like it's going to happen today."

She slapped him so hard he almost passed out. The pain radiated from his cheek and echoed down in his toes. Tears sprang to his eyes, and he balked.

"Don't ever say anything like that again." Her voice shook with a combination of fury and fear. "Understand me? Never."

In his mind's eye, there was a length of rope coiled on the top shelf of his closet. He'd tied the noose, looped the rope over the pull-up bar, tested his weight at the end of the loop—imagined the possibilities.

He thought about the pistol tucked under his bed back in London. Small, too small. It might not have been enough. He couldn't live with the acute agony of failure.

His focus shifted to the Millennium Bridge as he stood on

the ledge looking down at the Thames. How much water would he swallow before he stopped struggling? Would he choke on his own vomit? How painful would it be?

Too many questions.

"Jaybird."

He blinked. Back in the present, Melanie was looking at him. Her face was wet. He didn't deserve her tears.

"I'm sorry," he said.

He'd never tell her the rest.

Chapter Sixteen

THE HEART OF THE MATTER

Jay and Fleur sat in the lab, watching over Maia as she slept on the gurney. She'd been unconscious since her seizure.

Jay shivered in fear. He wanted her to wake up. No matter what happened, he knew he'd feel better if she just opened her eyes. Fleur said Maia hadn't lapsed into a coma, so that was a blessing.

Still, he wouldn't relax until she woke up.

"Do you know why she's worse off than me?" Jay asked.

Fleur pursed her lips. "More ill, you mean?"

"Yeah."

"I have some thoughts, hypotheses, and theories… nothing set in stone quite yet, I'm afraid." She rested her hand on his knee. Her touch was warm. "I'm not giving up on this."

"I believe you," he said.

No matter how hard he tried, Jay couldn't manage to push his doubts about Fleur to the back of his mind. He remembered what Melanie had said before about Fleur being dangerous. He didn't think she was, but how could he know for certain?

He got up from the couch and went to look at the rats. They looked still inside the cage, hardly moving at all. As he got closer, he saw they were sleeping. They struggled to breathe, and dried blood crusted the fur around their mouths.

What was wrong with them?

"Something the matter?" Fleur asked.

"The rats don't look so good," he said. "What kind of treatment have you been giving them?"

"No treatment," she answered. "They're the control."

"I thought they were getting the same treatment as us?"

She shook her head. "We needed a control."

Jay tried to remember the scientific method. He'd learned it in school, before the plague. Everything before the plague was centuries away. Based on what Fleur was saying, the control was the subject that didn't receive treatment.

It was all a big experiment.

"You're experimenting on us."

Her brow furrowed. "Pardon?"

"Me, Maia, and the rats. You're using us as test subjects."

"Only in a way," she said. "I'm still trying to cure you, after all."

"Why not try to cure the rats?"

"I want to make sure the treatment I'm giving you is working—that you're not just building up immunity. And the only way to measure that is against an unchanging variable, such as the rats."

Her words made sense. Still, Jay couldn't shake the feeling something was wrong.

Fleur never took time explaining their treatments. She gave them pills, injections, and exams without going into detail. He didn't know what was in the pills she had him swallow.

The more he thought about it, the less comforted he felt.

Fleur touched his face. "You trust me, Jay, don't you? Everything will be okay."

She might have been right. He was doing more worrying than resting.

Without her help, he wouldn't still be alive. She had his best interests at heart, didn't she?

Why couldn't he sit back and let her take the reins?

"You're right," he said. "I'm sorry. I know I'm in good hands."

"The very best," she said, leaning in to kiss him.

No matter how many times Fleur kissed him, Jay couldn't get over the way she tasted. Everything about her was a dream— from the pressure of her lips to the scent of her perfume.

She was everything he imagined being with a woman was like. She was silk and satin and fire and fervor. With every fiber of his being, he wanted to slide right into her.

His hands slid up her back, tugging at the clasp of her bra. He almost got it unfastened when an alarm on the bookcase went off.

Fleur got to her feet and sprinted across the room to turn it off.

Maia woke up, groaning, and rolled over to one side. "What's going on? What's with the alarm?"

"It's time to take your medicine," Fleur chirped.

The change in tone was staggering. The voice thick with sensuality had dissolved into syrupy sweetness. The abrupt switch almost turned Jay's stomach.

"How are you feeling?"

"Tired," said Maia. She propped herself up on her elbows. Her body trembled from the strain. "You should have let me sleep a little bit longer."

"You can go back to sleep after you take this," Fleur said.

She went over to the bookcase, took out several bottles, and uncapped the containers. Jay watched, transfixed, as she peered into one of the bottles, frowned, and replaced the cap.

That was the treatment he'd received. Why wasn't she using that bottle with Maia?

Fleur looked up as though she sensed Jay watching her. When their eyes met, blood rushed into her cheeks. He wasn't supposed to notice what she was doing. He could tell by the look on her face he'd caught her off guard.

"Jay," she said, "could you go across the hall and get Maia some water to take these pills with?"

He stared past her to the empty glasses sitting on the bookcase. Whenever they needed water, they grabbed a glass and refilled it at the bathroom sink. There was no need to go across the hall to get water for his sister.

"Really?"

If looks could kill, she would've murdered him. "Maia needs to take these pills."

"There's water here," he said. "You can just use the tap."

Fleur scrunched up her face. "Tap water isn't good with this medicine. Some of the metal alloys have a negative effect—"

"What are you getting at?" Jay asked.

His face flushed with anger. If she was lying to him, he was going to lose it. She hadn't done anything to break his trust yet, but her behavior with the bottles gave him pause. She was worth a second look.

The lines in Fleur's face smoothed themselves out like they'd never been there in the first place. "I have no idea what you're talking about."

They were playing a game for which Jay didn't know the rules. The stakes were clear, but he had no clue how to play. How could he take on Fleur if he didn't understand her? For some reason, she was intent on him leaving the room.

It had something to do with the pill bottles, which were taking her too long to consider.

The back of his throat burned. It had been a while since he'd coughed, but now the urge was overwhelming. Stress, he believed. He suppressed the urge and tried to focus on the task at hand.

"Fleur," he said.

"Dr. Devereaux," she corrected.

They locked eyes. Neither blinked.

"I can get the water myself," Maia said.

"No need," Jay said.

"Jay," Fleur said. "*S'il vous plaît.*"

Maia got down from the gurney. She smoothed her clothes. Under the fluorescent lighting, she looked almost ethereal. She'd gotten so pale her tiny blue veins showed through her skin. Even her hair looked limp and exhausted, a far cry from its springy self.

The longer he looked at her, the more the urge to cry pressed against the inside of his chest. If one of them didn't leave the room, he wasn't going to be able to maintain his composure.

Maia held her hand out to Fleur. "Give me the pill. I'll go across and get some water and then lie down. You can test Jay while I rest."

Fleur kept her eyes on Jay's as she dispensed the medicine to Maia.

Without another word, Maia closed her hand around the pill. Jay heard, rather than saw, her open the door, step out into the hallway, and shut the door behind her.

Once Maia was out of sight, Fleur let down her guard. She shook the pill bottle in Jay's face. "These have been keeping your sister alive. Why can't you be thankful?"

He was thankful, and he hadn't let her know enough. But still, her change in demeanor was strange. Something was going on with the medicine—he'd seen something she hadn't wanted him to. No matter how uncomfortable the situation was, he needed to get to the bottom of it.

"You're lying," he said. "There's something you're not telling us. Something about the pills."

Fury flashed in Fleur's eyes. "After everything I've done, you still can't bring yourself to trust me."

The accusation stung because it rang true. He didn't trust her. He knew he shouldn't trust her—after all, he hardly knew her—but somehow, guilt nagged the back of his mind when he considered it. He didn't like her having control over his feelings.

Memories flooded his mind: the fever, the ice bath, and the whispers she'd never repeat.

Three words with the power to topple a city.

Jay swallowed. Was that what everything came down to in the end? Was the heart of the matter the heart, of all things?

He relaxed his shoulders. "Do you remember what you said to me when I was in the bathtub?"

Her eyes narrowed, but the fury faded into caution. "Do you remember?"

Few people had uttered those words to him and meant it. Never anyone he'd seen in a romantic context. True, his fevered brain might have constructed the whole thing. It could all be a ruse. But when he was beside her, everything was real. With the way she looked at him, even in anger, there was no way those words couldn't be sincere.

"I do. Did you mean it?"

The silence stretched to a minute. The wait was agonizing. Each second, he worried he'd gotten it wrong—she hadn't told him she loved him, after all. Now, he could be making a fool out of himself.

"Did I mean it?" Fleur asked.

Jay took a breath. She was asking herself more than for clarification from him. He saw her face shift again, her expression molding into one of curious surprise. He'd never seen anything like it before. He didn't know what to say or do to her.

"Yes," she said. "Yes, Jay. I meant it."

"You meant it?"

"I love you."

The words hit him again like a splash of cold water. He knew he'd just been angry with her, but he wasn't angry anymore. In the wake of her confession, there was nothing but elation. His chest swelled again, but this time, it was with a mixture of pride and affection.

He could grow to love her, too, and he wanted to show her how grateful he was for everything she'd done to help him and Maia.

Before he could stop himself, Jay grabbed Fleur's waist, and kissed her hard enough to bruise.

She responded with equal enthusiasm and a fervor he hadn't anticipated. She raked her fingernails down his chest, hooking her fingers through his belt loops.

Jay deepened the kiss. He couldn't get over how much he loved to kiss her. Every time was like the first time. She was incredible.

She moved her hands to his zipper, and he hesitated. When he stopped kissing her, she took a step back. "If we're moving too fast, all you have to do is tell me. We don't have to do anything you don't want to."

That was the problem—he wanted to. He'd wanted to have sex with Fleur for a while, and it had been driving him crazy. If he couldn't escalate their situation, he was going to implode.

At the same time, sleeping with her was some form of betrayal. He still had feelings for Melanie. Even if she didn't seem intent on returning them anymore, there was no denying they were there.

In spite of everything he knew, he only ever wanted her.

Was that sentiment still true?

Fleur laced her fingers through his, lifted his hand to her mouth, and pressed her lips to his knuckles. The sensation sent shockwaves over the surface of his skin. "If you want me, I'm yours. That's all there is to it."

The time for rational thinking had come and gone with his health.

If the disease wanted to take his life, he had to give it the finger somehow. What better way to thumb his nose at death than by participating in the purest expression of life?

Before his courage failed him, Jay tightened his hold on Fleur and led her up the stairs to the loft. He was ready, and this time, there wouldn't be any distractions.

Chapter Seventeen

EASIER THAN THINKING

Lips on lips on necks on skin—everything hot and exciting and new.

For the first time, he saw what all the fuss was about.

Fleur was exquisite. How had he wanted anything with Melanie when she offered him so much more?

She took off his shirt. He pulled his over his head. Everything was happening so fast. He wanted to stop time and save it, or at least slow it down. There would only be one first time, after all. He wanted it to matter.

Jay rolled them over so he was on top and Melanie was underneath him.

Melanie.

He blinked. No, it was Fleur. Of course it was Fleur.

What was wrong with him?

Fleur took off her glasses. "Is something the matter?"

Jay took them from her and set them on the nightstand. "It's nothing. Just… give me a second."

She lowered the hand on his belt. "Take all the time you need. No reason to hurry."

She had a point, of course. But the longer they waited, the more anxious Jay became.

More than anything, he wanted Fleur. There was no denying that.

Why, then, had he pictured making out with Melanie?

"I'm not feeling well," he said.

"Why? Do you think your blood sugar is low?"

"No," he said. "It's not like that."

How could he put how he was feeling into words? He wasn't even sure how he was feeling. He couldn't define it. There were so few times in his life he'd been unable to identify his feelings.

Jay was aimless, lost, adrift—and there was nothing to grab onto.

Fleur touched his cheek. "Is it something other than the virus?"

"I don't know," he admitted.

It was the first time in a long time he'd been honest with her, and still, it felt like lying.

"I think you're just worried about Maia," Fleur said, "and I don't blame you. If my sister were sick, I'd be terrified. You're handling this better than I think I ever could."

She was trying to reassure him, but to Jay, her words rang hollow. She couldn't understand the agony he was in unless she'd lost her family, too. He didn't know much about Fleur, but something in her voice made him think she'd never felt such pain.

She rubbed her thumb across his cheek. "Let me help you. Please."

Against his better judgment, he leaned down and kissed her. Kissing her was easier than thinking, after all. The less thinking he did, the better off he'd be. Thinking was the source of so much of his unhappiness. Thinking caused him to fight with Maia, lie to Sean and shut out Melanie.

It was easier not thinking now that there wasn't as much blood in his head as other parts of his body.

He pulled away from Fleur to catch his breath.

Her face was flushed, her lips were swollen, and he had never wanted anything as much as he did her.

Maybe it was time to cross an item off his list.

The marvel of it all had been how fast it was over.

What had motivated people since the dawn of time, the act all the songs and poems were about—well, it hadn't lasted. As much fun as it had been, it was over in no time.

At first, he wasn't sure anything had even happened. It was like he'd been hit with the flat of a shovel, enveloped in a burst of light and spasming muscles.

After they had finished, Jay lay back against the pillows with Fleur's head resting on his chest. He worried his heartbeat would punch through her cheek. Her hair tickled his nose. He let it happen. He didn't feel like moving. If anything, he felt like crying, though that didn't make much sense.

Sex was nothing at all like he had imagined. He hadn't told Fleur he was a virgin because it was all over and done with before he could think. If she doubted his experience, she hadn't acted like it. She gave as good as she got, and he didn't have to ask to know he was not her first.

It didn't bother Jay that Fleur had been with other men. She wasn't with them anymore.

She'd chosen him, and here he was.

He wasn't leaving her anytime soon.

Fleur lifted her chin and kissed him. Although he couldn't understand it, it was clear she cared about him. He cared about her, too, but he wasn't quite sure he could say it was love. After all, they didn't know each other well. Most of the time they'd spent together had involved medical procedures, not make-out sessions.

But what they'd just done? That seemed like something stronger than two strangers together.

Whatever the future held for them, there was no denying they had a connection. Jay hadn't felt such strong ties to anyone before—not even Melanie.

Fleur rolled over to the other side of the bed. Jay studied the curve of her spine and the way the muscles in her back flexed as she picked her shirt up off the floor. She pulled it on, got up from the bed, and wandered around in search of her pants.

Jay sat up and pointed to the wad of fabric in the corner. She smiled and went to retrieve it.

"Where are you going?" he asked. "We can stay here for a while."

"I'll just be downstairs," she said.

That made sense. She was going across the hall to check on everyone. If Sean and Melanie weren't running around town, they'd be wondering what had happened to Jay.

Maia had said she was going to sleep, but if she'd woken up, she'd be wondering where her brother was, too. What would Fleur tell them; she'd been conducting some new tests on him?

"Why are you looking at me like that?" Fleur asked.

"Like what?"

She stepped into her pants. "Like I'm made out of stardust."

"Maybe you are."

That made her laugh. He half believed it, but he was more flattered than upset by her reaction. Whenever he made her laugh or smile or sigh, his pride swelled like a balloon.

"We're all made of stardust. Every one of us," she said.

Sometimes he forgot how much she knew about the universe. "Tell me all about it."

"Well," she said, "almost every element on Earth forms at the heart of a star. When the star explodes, the heavier elements end up together—elements like hydrogen, which makes up eleven percent of the human body."

Jay let out a low whistle. Fleur winked.

"Come back when you're finished," he said.

"Try and stop me," she replied.

Jay watched with a mixture of yearning and awe as Fleur disappeared down the stairs and out of sight.

When he first saw her that day in the streets, he never imagined getting so close to her. Then again, he'd never imagined getting so close to any other woman. Although he'd wanted to be with Melanie for a long time, had he planned to sleep with her?

He'd wanted his first time to be perfect, and knowing it never could be... he'd still be a virgin if he hadn't met Fleur.

He took his time dressing. Fleur said she'd be coming back, but he didn't know how long she planned to be across the hall. Plus, if Melanie, Sean, Maia, or all three of them came back with her, he wanted to be clothed. It would be strange enough for them to think he'd had sex without seeing him naked.

With Fleur gone, he'd lost his anchor. He was drifting again, aimless and codependent for the first time in his life. He wasn't sure he liked it. He wasn't sure he didn't.

A few more minutes passed. Jay's stomach cried out, furious. He hadn't eaten for quite some time. Regardless of what Fleur was telling everyone across the hall, he wanted food. Even if they watched him while he rummaged through the fridge, one bite of a sandwich would make it all worth it.

He went downstairs. His stomach growled, followed by a squeal.

Eeeeee.

Puzzled and alarmed, Jay pressed a hand against his gut. What kind of noise was that? He shrugged his worry off. Maybe he was just hungrier than he'd imagined.

He stepped off the last step. Again, he heard a squeal, louder this time.

Eeeeee!

It wasn't coming from his stomach. It was in the laboratory.

In another minute, he recognized the sound—the rats emitted similar squeaks whenever Fleur fed them. This time, though, the squeals sounded much more desperate.

Goosebumps rose on Jay's skin. Something was wrong.

He stepped into the lab to see what was happening. Fleur stood in front of the bookcase with her back to him. She hadn't gone to check up on Maia after all. The rat cage was in front of her.

A small, furry head poked out from her closed fist. A long, pink tail quivered from the bottom of her hand.

He wanted to say something to get her attention. He didn't know what she was doing, but he knew it wasn't good. She never held the rats, not even when she dosed them. The treatment they received got slipped into their food. And what was she doing squeezing that one? If she wasn't careful, she'd suffocate it.

"Fleur," Jay said.

She didn't move. She didn't even look at him.

"What are you doing?"

"Go back to bed. I'll be up in a minute."

"Fleur," he said, "please. Put the rat down."

"This is none of your concern. Just go upstairs, all right? I'll be up when I'm finished."

He took a step forward. "Finished with what?"

"I told you," she said. "It doesn't concern you."

Jay took another step forward. He was close enough to touch her. Standing that close, he could smell her perfume. The scent he'd grown to love was sickening now. His stomach clenched.

"They haven't been responding to the treatment," she said. "I don't know why, but they haven't. They're suffering, Jay. They're in so much pain." She turned to look at him, still holding the rat. The depth of sadness in her eyes surprised him. "Would you rather I let them live their last days in torment?"

"I don't know," he said. "What are you doing?"

Fleur closed her eyes. She squeezed the rat in her closed fist and covered its head with her other hand.

Jay tried to knock the rat out of her hand. She swiped something off the surface of the bookcase and jabbed it in his neck. The pain sent him reeling backward.

She was holding a syringe. The needle glinted in the light. The rat was still closed in her fist. He could see its tail wriggling around like a worm.

Jay turned his head and vomited. The acid stung his throat. Whatever Fleur had injected him with was already taking effect.

The edges of his vision softened and blurred. He felt his heartbeat in his fingers.

"What did you give me?"

"Doesn't matter," she said. "It'll all be all right."

Jay wiped his mouth with the back of his hand. He staggered forward, his knees buckled, and he fell hard on the tile. Pain flared up his thighs. His ribs were on fire.

Put down the rat, he thought. The words refused to make it from his brain across his tongue. *Put down the rat. Don't kill it. You can still find a cure like you did for me. Put down the rat, Fleur. Put down the rat.*

Fatigue ran him over like a runaway bus. He didn't have the strength to keep his head upright. The tile was cold against his cheek. It was hard to keep his eyes open, but he knew he had to try. Once he closed his eyes, he didn't know if he'd ever open them again. He didn't know what Fleur had done to him, but he was going to fight it as much as he could.

"Go to sleep," Fleur said. Jay wasn't sure whether she was talking to him or to the rat. "Close your eyes and it will all be over."

Sleep sounded divine. No matter how hard Jay struggled against exhaustion, it would win out in the end. Fleur had given him something strong. He was no match for its power.

Right before Jay's eyes fell closed, he saw the tail stop twitching.

Chapter Eighteen

HESITATION

Jay woke to the taste of blood. His tongue felt like a foreign object. His head throbbed and his legs ached. What was he doing on the floor? Had he fallen asleep or something?

He groaned and rolled over onto his side. Every muscle cried out in protest. His limbs felt like they weighed fifty pounds each. He didn't want to move again. It wasn't worth it. Whatever had happened to put him on the floor, it must have been powerful. He'd lost the fight.

There was an empty syringe lying on the tile several feet away from Jay. When his eyes hit the needle, everything came back— Fleur and the rats, the injection, the tail. Jay felt the overwhelming urge to puke again. There was nothing in his stomach. The best he could do was dry heave.

Once his nausea passed, Jay realized Fleur wasn't there. Where had she gone? Was she still in the apartment?

His first instinct was to call for her. Then, he remembered the rat and the way she'd squeezed it in her fist until the tail stopped twitching. She must have done the same thing to the other one. He wasn't sure he wanted to see her after knowing she'd done that. If she were capable of hurting an innocent animal, what would it be possible for her to do to him?

He'd underestimated Fleur. If he made the same mistake again, he doubted he'd wake up. She was a scientist—she knew what to do to get him to stop breathing. He was lucky she'd only dosed him with enough to knock him out. For the time being, he was thankful for the tiny bit of kindness she'd shown in sparing him.

Jay struggled to get up from the floor. The joints in his ankles creaked as he moved them. His muscles rebelled against the effort, especially the ones in his legs. He'd come down on the tile harder than he thought. Once he was upright, he clutched the edge of the gurney to stabilize himself. The world was spinning and he wanted it to stop as soon as possible.

As he stood there, catching his breath, his eyes fell on the open cage. The rats were missing. Fleur had put both of them out of their misery, and he had no idea what she'd done with their bodies after that. He felt sick again, but he knew he didn't have the time or strength to vomit.

He needed to move on. He had to tell somebody.

Fleur was still treating Maia. That treatment wasn't working, either. For all Jay knew, Fleur had strangled his sister while he slept.

He half-hobbled, half-ran to open the front door. His hands, slick with sweat, failed to grasp the sleek doorknob. He wiped them on his pants, muttered a curse, and twisted the metal The door swung open. He sprinted across the hall, through the open door, and into the kitchen.

His shins collided with a dining chair. He fell to the floor yet again.

He heard voices. Sean and Melanie.

"Maia," he said.

Sean knelt down beside him. "What the hell is wrong with you?"

"Where's Maia?" he asked.

"With the doctor," Sean said. "She's getting some blood. You all right there, mate?"

Jay couldn't speak. Maia was with Fleur. She could be killing her, and he'd never know.

"Melanie," he said. "Have you seen Maia?"

She knelt down next to Sean. "I was just in there with her. She's doing fine, Jay."

He didn't believe her. He wasn't sure who to trust anymore. The one person he trusted more than anyone was someone he knew next to nothing about. It hadn't turned out well for him. He didn't see a happy ending.

"Call the doctor," he said.

Sean and Melanie looked at each other. Maybe they thought he was losing his mind. Sean nodded, got up, and went back to the bedroom. Melanie sat on the floor and took Jay's hand in hers. He knew she meant it to be comforting, not romantic.

All it felt was sad.

"Dr. Devereaux said you were sleeping," she said. "Did you just wake up from a nightmare or something?"

He was living a nightmare. "I'm not feeling well."

"I can tell," she said. "You look bloody awful."

"Thanks." He squeezed her hand in what he hoped was a reassuring gesture. She didn't squeeze back. "Is Maia all right? Has anything happened?"

"She's fine, Jay. Relax. Getting sorted out now." She raised her hand to her mouth as though she wanted to kiss it. Instead, she let it fall back to the floor. "The doctor thinks you should go out for a walk later. You could use some fresh air."

"Come with me," he replied.

"She'll go with you, of course. No reason to worry. If anything happens, she'll be right there to help you."

To kill me, he thought. Put an end to my suffering.

"Melanie," he said. "I have to tell you something. It's about the doctor."

"What about me, Jay?"

His head snapped up so fast, he pulled a muscle in his neck.

Fleur knelt down beside Melanie. Sean stood back, watching, arms crossed over his chest. His face was hard to read, but Jay thought he saw concern in the lines of his expression.

Fleur, meanwhile, was smiling at him. It didn't reach her eyes. "I believe you were saying something about me."

His tongue felt oppressive like a weight inside his mouth. He couldn't move it. He was thankful.

There was nothing he could say to save himself from her.

"How's Maia?" Melanie asked.

Jay could've kissed her.

"She's doing okay. Not much to report." Fleur's smile faded. She cupped Jay's chin and turned his head from side to side. What was she looking for? "How are you feeling?"

"Fine," he replied without meaning a word.

"Good," she said. "That's good to hear."

Liar, he wanted to scream. *Liar, killer, psychopath*—but none of it came out. No matter how hard he tried, he couldn't force the words up from the back of his throat. The worst part was even if he could say what he was thinking, no one would believe him. He was the only person who knew about the rats. Even if they did believe him, she'd only killed some rats. Melanie had killed a rat when they were going through the Chunnel, so maybe it was nothing. Maybe he was paranoid and overreacting.

Then again, she had drugged him and left him alone.

"Let's get you off the floor and onto the couch," Fleur said. "Then, we'll take your temperature and see if anything has changed."

They both knew there was no need to take his temperature. He hadn't experienced any symptoms for a while. In fact, the vomiting earlier had nothing to do with the virus and everything to do with the rats. He doubted he was even contagious anymore.

Sean picked Jay up off the floor, sliding his arm around Jay's waist. Jay put his arm across Sean's shoulders and leaned on him. The room spun for a moment. He'd gotten up too fast, and he still hadn't had anything to eat. On top of that, he suspected there were side effects to the injection Fleur had given him.

With Fleur's help, Sean got Jay over to the couch. They laid him down and covered him up with a blanket. It was wool, scratchy and hot, and he didn't want anything to do with it. He let them put it on him anyway because it was easier than trying to fight. He needed to save the fight for when it mattered most. He wasn't sure what was happening, but he knew soon, he'd have to push back. He'd have to stop the doctor before she went too far.

Fleur handed him a glass of water from the kitchen. He looked right at her and asked Melanie to get him one.

Fleur pursed her lips, took a drink, and held the glass toward Jay. Still, he hesitated. He didn't trust anything that came from her.

"For the love of God," Sean said.

Jay accepted the water. He sipped it, watching Fleur for any signs he'd made a bad decision. If she were bluffing, her face didn't betray her. Was that how things would be between them from now on? If she didn't kill him, anxiety would.

"I want to talk to my sister," Jay said.

Melanie set another glass of water down on the coffee table. She stood next to Sean, and he put his arm around her. When she leaned into Sean, Jay's affair with her was over. She'd made her choice. He'd made his, too—except his choice might get him killed.

"I'll get her," Sean said.

Melanie grabbed his hand. "Wait, I'll go with you."

She cast a look at Jay before they headed down the hall. She was leaving him alone so he and Fleur could talk. Most likely, she thought she was doing him a favor. She'd never understand how terrified he was.

After Sean and Melanie had gone into the bedroom, Fleur moved Jay's legs off the couch and sat down beside him. He sprang up. She latched onto his wrist and squeezed it hard enough to bruise.

"Sit down," she hissed.

Jay sat back down. The menace in her voice was nothing like he'd ever heard. How had he gone so long without seeing this side of her?

How had she managed to fool him, to fool them all?

What did she have planned now?

"I'm going to ask you some questions," she said. "I want you to answer yes or no for each one. There's no need to talk—just nod or shake your head. Do you understand?"

This wasn't the woman he thought he'd been falling in love with. Jay didn't know if something had happened to Fleur or if he was finally seeing past her façade. Either way, the change in her demeanor terrified him.

He'd have to play along or risk getting hurt.

Foreboding trickled down Jay's spine. He wanted to run as far away from her as possible.

Even so, he nodded.

"*C'est magnifique*. Magnificent. Here's the first question: are you angry with me?"

What the hell did she expect? He scowled at her and nodded.

"Good. That's logical. Are you worried about Maia?"

Once again, he nodded.

"Afraid I'll hurt her?"

Hesitation. How was he supposed to answer? He didn't want her to know how much she intimidated him. She might use that to her advantage. Still, she knew the answer.

What would happen if he lied? Would she punish him for it?

"Answer me, Jay."

He shook his head.

She grabbed his chin again and raked her nails across his cheek. It stung.

"I saved you from the brink of death. I can bring you back there. Is that what you want?"

Do it. I dare you. He bit his tongue. He shook his head.

This was not the time for boldness. Maia needed help. Like it or not, Fleur was their best hope for a cure.

He had to play along until his sister was safe.

"Good boy," Fleur said. She moved her hand to cup the side of his face and kissed the gashes her nails had made in his cheek.

155

"How are we going to explain this mess, I wonder? Should we say you attacked me, and maybe I fought back? Or perhaps it had something to do with your fall. What do you think?"

"I trust you," he said. What the hell did she want?

"Glad you're finally learning." She kissed him on the mouth. "Now, there's something I think you should know about Maia."

His lips burned from her kiss. Bile crept up in his throat. "What did you do to her?"

"Not me, it's the virus."

Terror seized his gut. "What's wrong with her? What happened?"

Melanie's scream echoed from the end of the hallway. Jay leaped up from the couch.

Sean poked his head out of the bedroom. "Maia's unresponsive. We thought she was sleeping, but I can't find a pulse."

Jay looked at Fleur.

Her expression was blank.

Chapter Nineteen

SWEETNESS

Jay turned on Fleur, eyes blazing. "What did you do to her?"

"Not me," she said, "the virus. We've been through this, Jay. have yours and Maia's best interests at heart."

Jay sprinted toward the hallway. He tripped on a corner of the area rug and braced a hand against the wall to keep himself from falling. The apartment swirled around him.

"Careful," said Fleur.

"Help me," he said. It killed him to ask for help from her, of all people, but he didn't have a choice. There was no way he could save his sister on his own. "I don't know what to do for her."

Fleur got up from the couch. She walked over to Jay and put her hand on his back. It took all his willpower not to recoil when she touched him. "Run across the hall and grab her pills," she said. "It's the bottle with the blue cap. You know the one. Hurry."

I can't run, he wanted to argue. *I can barely stand.* But there was no point—he had to go get the medicine because the doctor was going to make sure Maia didn't die.

How long had Maia had been unresponsive. How long had Fleur waited to tell him what was wrong with her?

Rage simmered beneath the surface of his fear. Once Maia got better, he was going to kill Fleur.

Jay brushed her hand off and ran across the hall as fast as he could. The movement made his head swim and his lungs work overtime. Once he crossed the threshold to the laboratory, he slumped against the gurney.

His breath came in short, sharp pants. He wanted to throw up again. Again, there was no time.

He needed to save Maia.

Pills, he reminded himself. He had to find the bottle, the one with the blue cap. It was the same bottle he'd seen Fleur handling not too long before they'd had sex. The more he thought about it, the more he realized she'd used sex to distract him. He'd been on to something, something big.

Now, she wasn't there to stop him from investigating further.

Jay located the bottle on the bookcase. His hand hovered over it. What if he was playing right into her hands? She'd sent him to fetch the bottle, after all. Maybe she suspected he'd want to investigate. Of course, there wasn't time—the longer he stayed across the hall, the less safe it was for Maia.

Fleur was with her now. He didn't know what she was doing. He had to get back there as fast as he could.

He closed his hand around the bottle and spun on his heel. His heart was destroying the inside of his chest, but he knew he had no time to stop and catch his breath.

He had to keep moving. He had to save Maia.

Before he crossed the hall again, he needed to see what was inside the bottle. His pills and Maia's were in separate bottles, but he had no idea why. What did hers even look like?

Before he could stop himself, he pried off the blue cap and let it fall to the floor. It was filled with small, white capsules—pills that looked the same as his. He turned the bottle over and poured one into his hand. It looked exactly like the one he'd taken hours ago.

On a whim, he cracked the capsule open. Fine white powder spilled over his palm.

He raised his hand to his mouth, stuck his tongue out, and brushed it over the contents of the capsule.

It was sweet.

He reared back, stunned, and resolved to try again. This time, he tried a lot more of the powder.

Sweetness. Sweet like candy, like ice cream—

Like sugar.

Fleur was giving Maia sugar pills.

She'd gotten a placebo.

The muscles in Jay's body locked up in sheer fury. He clenched his jaw so hard he felt a nerve jerk in his neck. Pure, unadulterated rage flowed through his veins.

What the hell was going on? What had she done to Maia?

Fleur's face appeared in his mind's eye. He wanted to destroy it beyond recognition. If someone gave him a baseball bat, he would break every bone in her body without a second thought.

Who did she think she was? What gave her the right to choose who lived or died? Why hadn't she given Jay the placebo pill instead?

I promise you I'm going to do everything I can to save your sister, Jay.

In a fit of righteous anger, he threw the bottle across the room. It hit the wall and tiny capsules went flying everywhere. Jay watched, breathing heavily, as things fell into place. Fleur had been lying the entire time. She knew why Jay was responding better to the treatment—he was the only one getting the treatment.

For whatever reason, she'd chosen not to help Maia. She didn't seem troubled that Maia might die.

Whatever it takes, I want her to live.

Everything made perfect, infuriating sense.

The scream that had been building up inside of him burst out. He dashed across the hall, threw open the door, and shouted Fleur's name. When she didn't answer, he ran down the hall into the open bedroom.

Maia's sleeping body lay on top of the covers. Melanie sat next to her, holding her hand. Sean stood next to Fleur, who was shining a flashlight into Maia's eyes.

"Jay," Fleur said, "did you bring the pills?"

I hope you don't think I'm deliberately keeping anything from you.

"Bitch," Jay spat. "Placebo? What the hell is wrong with you?"

Sean stood between them. "Easy there, mate."

"Don't 'easy there, mate' me. She's a liar and a fraud." He took a step forward. Sean stood his ground. "Step aside, Sean."

"You're scared," he said. "Don't do this. You're going to regret it."

"The only thing I regret right now is trusting her," Jay said.

The more he thought about it, the more betrayed he felt. He'd kissed Fleur, touched her, slept with her—she'd even said she loved him. How much of that had been a lie?

You have my word.

His chest bumped Sean's. Neither of them backed down. "Don't make me fight you. My issue's with her."

Sean grabbed Jay's arm. Jay shoved him. Sean swore and shoved him back.

"Jay," Melanie said. "Please, calm down."

"Is she breathing?" Jay demanded.

"Is who breathing?"

"Maia!"

Melanie held her hand above Maia's face. "Yes."

Jay relaxed, but only a little. He was still angry with Fleur. When he turned back around, Sean hadn't moved. Jay pulled his arm back and curled his hand into a fist.

I will never lie to you about your sister's condition.

"Move or I'll punch you."

"Punch me," Sean said.

His knuckles cracked against Sean's jaw. Pain exploded in his hand. He'd made a bad call. His fingers went numb. Maybe he'd broken them.

"Jesus," Sean wiped blood from his mouth. "What the hell has gotten into you?"

"She has," he replied.

I hope you don't think I'm deliberately keeping anything from you.

Sean glared at him. "Dr. Devereaux saved your life, mate. You were half-dead when we got out of the Chunnel." He rubbed his jaw and winced. "She saved Maia, for Christ's sake."

You have my word. I will never lie to you about your sister's condition.

Jay's anger flared again. "She's killing Maia." He pushed Sean out of the way and stormed toward the doctor. One hand dug into her waist; the other squeezed her throat. "I know about the pills."

"*Merde,*" she breathed.

Sean started forward. Fleur held up a hand to stop him.

"He'll kill you," Sean said.

"I don't think so." Even with Jay's hand around her throat, she didn't look frightened—she looked sad. "He's waiting for answers. He needs me alive."

Fleur was right, and they both knew it. Even if he wanted to, Jay couldn't kill her yet. His thoughts were tangled up like a string inside his head. How much longer would he have to wait for them to come unraveled?

"You've been giving Maia a placebo," he said.

"Christ alive," Sean said.

Melanie gasped.

Fleur grabbed Jay's wrist. "All for the sake of the experiment. Without a placebo, there is no control."

The sake of the experiment. She didn't care about Maia. She didn't care about Jay. She didn't care what happened to either of them. All that mattered to her was the scientific method.

Why had she told him she loved him? If she didn't care about him, then why had she insisted? He needed to know. He had to hear her say it.

"Why did you tell me you loved me?" he asked.

"You needed to hear it," Fleur replied. "I had no idea how much time you had left." She applied pressure to his wrist, but he didn't let up. "I might have learned to mean it, Jay. What do you think?"

He thought she was a liar and a cheater and a fraud. He thought she was a bitch. He wanted her to suffer—the way she'd made him suffer. He wanted to hold out hope to her before dashing it against the rocks.

Then and only then would she know what he was thinking.

"Did you kiss me for the same reason?" Jay asked. "What about the sex? Was that part of your plan?"

Melanie choked. She was the only person besides Jay who knew about the list. She knew what he wanted to check off. She might have thought she'd be his first.

For both of their sakes, he wished she had been.

"I would do it all again," Fleur said. "Didn't it make you happy, even for a moment? Didn't you forget about the virus for a while?" Her eyes searched his for affirmation. Even now that he knew what she was capable of, Jay wanted to reassure her. Had she had his happiness in mind the whole time after all? "You're hurting me, Jay. Can't we stop this for now? Your sister needs my help."

At the mention of his sister, Fleur renewed Jay's fury. His hand jumped from her waist to join the other on her neck. His brain was on fire.

There was no stopping now.

Fleur's hands found his wrists. Her eyes locked on his. He still saw sadness in them, maybe doubt, but he still didn't see the one thing that would've stopped him—fear.

She wasn't afraid, and he hated her for it. He wanted to give her a reason to fear. He needed her to understand what hopelessness was like.

Jay brought his hands together until Fleur started choking. Sean yelled something, but the throbbing of his heartbeat in his ears drowned it out. Melanie screamed his name. Fleur thrashed in his grip. Her face turned red.

He thought of what had happened since arriving in Calais—meeting Fleur, starting treatment, fighting with Sean, holding Melanie, sneaking around with Fleur—it had all made sense in some way.

But then came the deception and the awfulness began— Maia's seizures, the relapse, Fleur killing the rats, the cold prick of a needle as it slid into his neck—

In the present, Fleur gagged.

Jay squeezed harder.

The unfairness of it all was that nothing would change. Even if he killed Fleur, he knew he'd still be miserable. Maia wouldn't heal. There was a chance she could die.

If he murdered Fleur, then the cure would die with her. He'd kill the possibility that Maia would survive.

Jay let go of Fleur just as her face turned purple. She fell to the floor in a heap, unconscious.

Melanie swore and ran over to her. She squatted down and grabbed Fleur's wrist, checking for a pulse. Once Sean knew Fleur was alive, he latched onto Jay's arm.

"You pull that shite again," he said, "at least give us a warning."

Chapter Twenty

THE DREAM IN RUINS

After a few minutes, Jay's anger had subsided, replaced by resignation. He couldn't kill Fleur. No matter how much she'd done to hurt him, he still had to cooperate. She was the only person capable of saving Maia.

Beside him, Sean's breathing came in ragged pants, and his face was flushed. What did he think they should do about Fleur?

"I don't think I really could've murdered her," Jay said once he'd caught his breath.

"I know," Sean said, "and I hate her, too. That doesn't change the fact we need her to save Maia."

"She's out cold," said Melanie, still stooped over Fleur. "Not sure when she'll wake up or if she'll wake up at all."

Sean nodded grimly. If Fleur died, there would be no hope for a cure. "What about Maia?"

Melanie left Fleur and got back on the bed with Maia. If Maia had moved any, Jay couldn't tell. Melanie pressed her fingers to the side of Maia's neck.

Jay held his breath. He prayed.

"Still out, but alive. If she doesn't wake up soon, she might have lapsed into a coma."

Jay climbed onto the bed on the other side of Maia. He tapped his sister's cheek. It was clammy.

"Wake up, Maia," he said.

"What are you doing?" Melanie asked.

"What does it look like? I'm waking her up. No way in hell she's going into a coma."

"You don't get it, Jaybird. It might not make a difference."

He touched Maia's face again. Her skin felt the same as it always had. If she were dying, wouldn't it feel different somehow? Wouldn't there be some way he would be able to tell? She couldn't slip away without him knowing, could she?

He didn't want to lose the only family he had left. The only way he'd survived losing his parents was with Maia by his side.

Without conscious effort, Jay thought back to the funeral. They'd waited until both their parents were dead—it was easier, more economical. Per government order, they'd both been cremated. The urns sat in an empty coffin—they could only borrow one as a result of high demand. When the ceremony finished, Jay and Maia took the urns to Tower Bridge. They scattered ashes in the Thames, tears dripping down their faces and mingling with the river.

In that moment, they were closer than they had ever been. Jay wondered if the two of them could be that close again.

The snap of Sean's fingers brought him back to the present. "You said a lot of things about Dr. Devereaux. Do you think they're all true?"

"How can I get you to believe me?" Jay asked.

"I want to, mate." Sean looked at Melanie. "What do you think?"

"He might be mental," she said, "but I've never seen him that angry before, especially over something that didn't really happen." Her attention moved to Jay. "It's worth investigating, wouldn't you agree?"

"Good enough for me," Sean said.

He walked over to the bed and held his hand out. Jay took it and let Sean help him get back on his feet. He brushed off his clothes, even though he didn't need to, and waited for Sean to say something else.

Melanie spoke instead. "Where can we find out what's up with the doctor?"

Jay racked his brains and tried to come up with a plan of action.

They needed to investigate, but what could they look into? Was there anywhere Fleur could've slipped up somehow, anything to help clue them to her true self?

He remembered standing in the lab not too long ago, asking Fleur if he could see her credentials. She'd led him to them, proudly—she'd gone to Oxford, for God's sake. He'd seen the diplomas.

But were they all real?

Jay looked at the wall. The framed diplomas were all still there above the headboard, staring him down as they awaited inspection. In that moment, it was clear what they had to do.

"She showed me these diplomas." Jay pointed to them. "I didn't look too closely. Now might be the time."

"Take Maia into the bathroom," Sean told Melanie. "Try putting her in the tub and turning on the shower. The water might help her wake up."

Melanie started to ease Maia off the bed. "What are we going to do about Fleur?"

"Leave her," Sean said. "We have more pressing business."

"Wait," Jay said. "I'll help you, Mels."

He scooped Maia into his arms. She weighed next to nothing—her lightness shocked him. He carried her, bridal-style, into the bathroom and tried not to focus on how sick she looked up close.

Melanie turned on the tap and sat on the edge of the tub while it filled up. She was silent.

Jay laid Maia on the tile floor, careful not to bump her head. He touched the hem of her shirt, frowning. "You'll take her clothes off, won't you? If she gets these wet, she might catch a cold later."

Once the words left his mouth, he realized what he'd said. It wouldn't make a difference if Maia caught a cold—she was already dying, and she had been for a while. He felt a twinge of foolishness mingled with fear.

He worried, more than anything, that he would lose his sister. Even armed with the knowledge she'd taken a placebo, he wasn't sure he could save her. They could try treating her with his medicine, but she hadn't built up any tolerance to it.

The so-called cure could kill her in the weak state she was in.

Melanie turned the water off. "Jay, love, I'm so sorry."

He couldn't bring himself to look away from Maia's face. He loved her more than he could say. She meant the world to him and more. They'd been there for each other for as long as he remembered.

If he lost her, he'd be losing a piece of his soul.

How could he put that depth of sadness into words?

"I should go back in there and help Sean," he said.

Jay lifted Maia's hand to his mouth and kissed the back of it.

"She's in good hands," said Melanie.

"I know," he said. "Thank you."

Jay let go of his sister and headed for the door.

Melanie reached him in two short strides. She took his face in her hands, drew him down to her, and kissed him on the lips. The way she did it told him exactly what she meant—she almost didn't need to say it. He meant a lot to her, and she needed him to know. The kiss wasn't romantic as it might have been once. Instead, Jay drew strength and comfort from it.

"I love you," she said, "and I don't want you to forget it. No matter what happens, you'll always have me. You're family, Jay. Do you understand?"

He did understand, and the truth broke his heart. He didn't think he'd ever been so loved in all his life. No matter what happened to him or to Maia, he knew he could always count on them. Melanie was right—she and Sean weren't just his friends.

Somewhere along the way, they had become his family.

"I love you, too," he said. "Take care of her."

"You know I will."

He took another long look at Maia before heading back to Fleur's bedroom. To his surprise, she was still unconscious on the floor.

167

Sean stood on the bed. He ripped a frame from the wall, nail and all, and tossed it onto the duvet. It joined the pile of others. The glass was broken in a few of them. Blood dripped onto the pillows.

Jay looked up and noticed the cuts in Sean's hands. "Slow down. You're bleeding."

"From the glass," he said, "or the nails. I don't know anymore." He reached for another diploma, this one in a gilded frame, and tore it from the wall. "Look at those down there. What do you see?"

Jay picked up a frame. The glass was cracked. What was he supposed to be looking for? Sean had gone crazy.

"Get closer," Sean said. "Press your nose against the glass."

Jay did. At first, he didn't see anything odd—a flat piece of paper with flat words and a flat seal, nothing worth breaking glass over.

Then, it hit him—flat, flat, flat.

Calligraphy was raised. Seals should be, too.

Fleur had framed a printout.

She hadn't been to Oxford.

She was a fraud.

Jay threw the diploma across the room until it hit the wall. The wooden frame splintered and fell apart. The glass shattered.

Liar!

The dream was in ruins, and he was awake.

"Fleur!"

Her name erupted from his mouth like the cry of a wild animal. He wanted to hurt her. He wanted to scream.

The lies kept piling up. There was no reason for it—she was lying because she could.

"Everything she told us was a lie," Sean said. "She isn't even a doctor. I don't know what she is."

Jay felt suffocated by the intensity of his anger. Never in his life had he wanted to kill someone like he wanted to kill Fleur. He'd already come close to succeeding once. Now that Sean knew the extent of her betrayal, maybe he wouldn't want to stop Jay this time. And she was still unconscious. It would be so easy.

He dropped to his knees on the bedroom floor. Sean got down from the bed, went over to him, and put a hand on his shoulder. "Whatever you're thinking, it's not worth it, mate."

"She lied to me," Jay said. "She lied to everyone."

"I know," Sean replied, "but we can't do anything about it. We need her, Jay. Maia's still sick."

"Because of her," he spat.

"Yes, but she cured you. Maybe she's the only one who can help Maia now, too."

In spite of his anger, he knew Sean was right. Fleur had managed to save Jay's life. She might be able to save Maia's. Regardless of how she presented herself, she was their best hope for Maia's survival. He loved his sister more than anything. He would do whatever it took to keep her alive.

"She slept with me," Jay said.

"You told us."

"She said she loved me, Sean. I thought I loved her, too."

"Jesus," Sean breathed. "You can't just dump this shite on me out of nowhere, Jay. I didn't even know you fancied her. You don't tell me anything anymore—not since we left London."

It had been longer, and they both knew it. Jay had lied to Sean since discovering he was sick. He thought he'd been keeping his friends safe by lying to them, but maybe he was wrong. His deception made the tension worse. Fleur had lied, too, perhaps even to protect them. He wasn't sure he could forgive her for what she'd done to Maia, but he couldn't condemn her when he was guilty, too.

Jay swallowed the lump in his throat. He wasn't sure what to say. The situation needed something, but he didn't know what. He got up from the floor and shoved his hands in his pockets.

Sean leveled his gaze. "Melanie told me about everything, Jay— about the two of you, I mean."

His heart sank like a rock. "Everything? You mean it?"

"Yeah," he replied. "I've known for a while. She started acting flighty right before you told us Maia was sick. Figured she wanted out."

Jay nodded. Sean and Melanie had had some disagreements. He'd probably seen it coming.

"You didn't say anything to me," Jay said.

"What would have been the point? You're my best mate." He shrugged. "If she's going to cheat on me with someone, I'd rather it be you. After all, I know you—"

Melanie screamed.

Sean's voice died in this throat. Jay turned and sprinted into the bathroom. Melanie was in the tub, fully clothed and straddling Maia. Maia's head lolled to one side, bobbing in the water. Her eyes were closed. Melanie slapped her cheeks, muttering what sounded like a prayer.

"She isn't responding," Melanie said.

"It's a coma," Sean replied. "We need to get the doctor."

With Fleur's help, the three of them managed to get Maia out of the bathtub. Fleur slipped a silk robe on her and didn't bother to tie it. None of that mattered anymore.

They set Maia down on Fleur's bed again. Fleur ducked out of the room to fetch some medical equipment, leaving the trio alone with Maia. She looked so close to death that Jay couldn't look at her anymore. Melanie sat on the edge of the bed, holding Maia's hand.

Sean paced the length of the bedroom and muttered prayers to a God he didn't believe in. Jay appreciated it all the same. He sat down beside Melanie and put his arm around her. His eyes burned as though he were going to cry. He wasn't sure he had the strength.

"You can cry," she said. "It's okay for you to cry after something like this."

She was trying to comfort him, but he still didn't think he could release the pain inside of him. Rage and grief and terror had been building up in him since discovering Fleur was giving Maia a placebo. If anything else happened to Maia, he was going to kill Fleur with his bare hands. He'd jump on her and strangle her and watch the life leave her eyes. He'd never wanted to hurt an animal, let alone another human, like he wanted to hurt her.

The more he thought about Maia's condition, the more infuriated he became.

"I want to," he said.

"Then do it."

"I can't."

Sean stopped pacing. He came over to the bed and sat down on the other side of Jay. He put his arm around his shoulders.

For the first time in a long time, the three of them united. Their bodies formed an unbreakable chain.

Jay hung his head. He was full of emotion he couldn't quite name.

"She'll wake up," Sean said.

"But what if she doesn't?"

"She will, Jay. She has to."

He couldn't look at Sean anymore, either. They both knew Maia's health was not a guarantee. Based on the growth of her illness, no one could imagine what might happen going forward. Not even Fleur seemed to understand what was happening to her.

Fleur came back into the room. She dropped a stethoscope, a syringe, and several other things onto the duvet.

Jay leaped up right away. "What can I do to help?"

"Nothing," she said. "Get out of my way."

Her cold response burned him. That was his sister, his family, and she wouldn't let him help? She was crazy to think he wouldn't do whatever it took to keep Maia alive.

"Just tell me what to do and I'll do it," he said.

"I am," she replied. "Get the hell out of here."

Sean stood next to Jay. "He wants to help. Let him."

"He's emotional and he'll only get in my way." Fleur picked up the stethoscope and put the ends in her ears. "If you all want to help me, you'll get some air. There's nothing anyone but me can do for her right now. Take a breather while you can."

"She's not out of the woods yet," Jay said.

"We can come right back." Sean's eyes searched Jay's, imploring him to reach an understanding. "If we stay here, we'll be a nuisance. One quick walk, and we'll be back. Maybe by then the doctor will have got it sorted out."

Jay didn't think anyone could "get it sorted out." It was un-sort-out-able. None of them had any real control over what happened to Maia next. Beyond prayer, there was nothing they could offer for her healing. The helplessness bothered Jay the most. He hated knowing there was nothing more he could do for his sister.

"Jay?" Sean asked.

"I don't want to leave her here alone with Maia." He glared at the doctor. "I don't trust her."

Fleur ignored the dig and pressed the stethoscope's metal disc against Maia's chest.

"Melanie," Jay said, "would you mind staying here? I know she'll be okay as long as you're around."

"I'd love to," she said.

"Good then. It's settled." Sean patted Jay's back. "You ready then, mate?"

Jay watched his sister as she slept, wondering when and if she was going to wake up. Although she looked paler and weaker than she had not long before, she was still the same Maia. He felt the overwhelming urge to kiss her sweaty forehead but decided against it. Now wasn't the time.

The sooner they went out, the sooner he and Sean could come back and see her again.

He nodded.

Sean jerked his head in the direction of the door. "Lead the way, mate."

"We'll be in the lab when you get back," Fleur said. "There's more room in there, and all my equipment. Just come there when you get in. We'll take care of her."

"Thank you," Jay said.

Sean clapped him on the shoulder. They headed down the hallway, and out the front door. Everything would be all right. Fleur couldn't be trusted, but Melanie could. She was going to be there to watch over Maia.

No matter what happened, it was going to be fine.

Chapter Twenty-One

ONE QUICK WALK

They headed all the way down to the water. For all the time they'd spent in Calais, they'd never really taken the time to appreciate the English Channel. They had so many other things to worry about. Seagulls careened in lazy circles overhead, punctuating the still, salty air with their cries. The sun played hide-and-seek behind thick, gauzy clouds tinged gray on the bottom. There, on the beach, the virus seemed so far away. In the fresh air, perhaps, they would get a fresh start.

Sean spoke first. "Been through a lot, haven't we? You and me."

"Yeah, man," Jay said. "I mean, more than most people."

"Sometimes it feels like we've been friends for ages."

"Maybe we have been."

"In another life, maybe."

They were both quiet for a minute. Jay focused on the crashing of the waves against the shoreline. Even in such an uncertain world, tides rose and fell like normal.

"I'm sorry I didn't tell you," Jay said.

"It's okay."

"I should have..." Should have what? How could he put it into words? "I should have said something."

"Listen," Sean broke in, "I said it's okay."

"I wasn't going to tell Melanie. She walked in on me puking. That's the only reason I told her before you found out. I'd never straight up—"

"Jay, stop. All right? Stop."

He gripped Jay's upper arms, pulling both of them to a halt. His green eyes searched Jay's. Up close, there were flecks of gold around his pupils. Had they ever been so close before? Every muscle in Jay's body tensed. Was he supposed to pull away? Was he supposed to stand still?

"Sean," Jay said. "Hey, buddy. You there?"

After a minute, Sean let go of Jay and took a step back, wiping his palms on his thighs. He laughed, but it was shaky. Jay didn't laugh with him.

"Let's keep going," Sean said. "Talk about something else."

The two of them resumed walking. Jay shortened his strides so it was easier for Sean to keep up with him. Maybe it was best to pretend nothing had changed between them, that the conversation hadn't shifted somewhere uncomfortable, somewhere Jay didn't want to go.

"How did you find out about your family? Did they just tell you they were sick?"

"Usual way, I s'pose. Mom lost her energy, stopped eating as much. Cold turned into coughing up blood. You know the drill." Sean kicked a pebble across the sand. "Dad went next, same thing, and then my sister. Truth be told, sometimes I wonder if she didn't lose her will to live a little. If maybe it hurt her too much to think of going on without them, so she didn't bother." He exhaled, breath making steam in the cool air. "Not even for my sake."

Jay sucked in a breath. "She didn't kill herself, did she?"

"No, but she might as well have. Wouldn't eat, wouldn't drink, even asked me to kill her a couple of times." He let out a low whistle. "Sometimes I wish I had. Maybe then, she wouldn't have suffered."

"Jesus, Sean. I didn't know."

"No way you could have."

Jay stooped to pick up a rock. "I never even asked."

"You didn't need to ask," Sean said.

"We talked so many times," Jay said. "I thought we knew each other."

"We do."

"Maybe once we did." He rubbed the back of his neck. "But no, not anymore."

"No. Not anymore."

Another silence stretched between them. Jay pitched the rock into the water, standing still until it disappeared beneath the waves. Standing by the water reminded him how small he was, how powerless. But what was it Fleur had said? *We're all made of stardust. Every one of us.* How could he be as immense and powerful as the stars when standing by a lot of water made him feel so tiny?

"I should've told you about Fleur. About me and Fleur. The whole thing."

Sean stopped walking. Jay turned around and looked at him.

Sean's expression softened. "You didn't have to, mate. You're allowed one secret."

"I shouldn't still be keeping secrets. Maia made me promise, and with you and Mels, I guess I just—"

"Jay," Sean said, "you really need to learn to let things go."

Jay gave him a watery smile. "Yeah. I guess I do."

The darkening clouds rolled in across the sun, blocking it as it dipped into the water. The seagulls were silent, having disappeared wherever seagulls went once the sun went down. Between the clouds, fingers of gold and orange stretched across the sky. The boys looked up at the sunset, saying nothing. How long had it been since Jay had watched a sunset? How long had it been since he'd taken the time to take a breath, to really mull things over?

"Maia used to say sunsets were proof there was a God." Jay kept his eyes on the horizon as the moon came up. "I wish she could see this."

"She will," Sean said.

"Not this one."

Sean sniffed. He stooped down to pick up a pebble, which he slipped into Jay's hand. "Throw it, mate. Aim for the moon."

"What good will that do?"

"I dunno," Sean said. "Only one way to find out."

Jay looked out over the water, squinting in the faint light. Then, he pulled his arm back and launched the rock into the sea. When it disappeared into the inky blackness of the night, he felt more like himself.

"Nice, innit? Normal." Sean grinned at him. "Yeah?"

"Yeah," Jay echoed. "Normal."

"Better go back now. The gang might be worried."

Jay nodded. There was nothing else to say, nothing left unsaid, no more rift to repair. He slung his arm around Sean's shoulders, and in the fading light, under the cover of the clouds and the faint moon poking through, they headed back to the apartment.

For the first time in a long time, everything was fine.

They were gone for longer than Jay realized. As they opened the door to the lab, moonlight poured into the hallway. He didn't see Fleur or anyone else. Maia wasn't on the gurney—maybe she was in the loft.

For some reason, the sheet of paper hanging over the gurney lay crumpled on the floor. He thought he saw blood on the corner of it. Maybe it was just a trick of the light.

"I'm going to go see if they're across the hall," Sean said.

Jay nodded. "I'll look around here."

He went farther into the apartment and went over to the couch.

That was when he saw something that turned his blood to ice.

The light was all wrong. The curtains were open, and the full moon cast an unfamiliar shadow on the floor. It looked like Maia's sleeping form, but he couldn't find her profile. The silhouette of her head was large and bulky and he couldn't see her nose no matter how hard he tried.

It didn't make sense.

He took a step forward into the room. Goosebumps pulled the hair on his arms toward the ceiling.

He took another step toward the bed. Stomach acid crept up the back of his throat.

Maia lay on her back with a pillow on her face.

She never slept on her back, especially not on the couch. And even if the moon were bright, she wouldn't have covered her face with a pillow. If anything, she would've gotten up and shut the curtains first.

As Jay crept toward his sister, fear bubbled up inside him. Something was wrong, but he didn't want proof. Whatever had happened to Maia while he was gone, he wanted to keep it out of his mind. He didn't want it to exist.

He wanted to curl up in a ball and crawl away from the uncertain future.

As long as he stayed at a distance from Maia, he'd be able to pretend everything was fine. The minute he stepped forward, he would shatter the illusion.

He took a deep breath and made his move. Now that he was close enough to touch her, he lifted the pillow off of her face. The moonlight struck her cheek.

She didn't look right.

He took a step closer and turned on the lamp.

His stomach clenched.

Maia was still. She wasn't just resting—she was frozen, like a statue. Like something inanimate.

Her eyes had fallen shut. Blood crusted at the edges of her parted lips. Dried blood caked under her nose. Her entire face looked swollen.

The pillow tumbled from Jay's fingers. He reached out with shaking hands and pried her right eye open. The whites were bloodshot, the pupils cloudy and unfocused.

He tried the other eye and got the same result.

His blood heated and cooled in alternating waves.

The world had ended and the afterlife was closing in on him. He screamed, and what came out of him was nothing close to human.

Jay is four and his sister is playing with him. They sit in a patch of sunlight streaming from the kitchen window. Their parents moved the table against the wall to give them plenty of room. Maia drapes a sheet over it to create a makeshift cave. She crawls into it, laughing, and growls like a bear. Jay doesn't realize the noise is coming from his sister. Before he knows why, he bursts into tears.

Maia is out and at his side in an instant. She holds him and rocks him just like their mother does. She tells him she's sorry. As he will always do, and in that moment, he forgives her.

Jay is seven and his family has gone out on the water. They're on a boat with someone—he can't remember who—and he might be afraid of the river. Maia, wise beyond her sullen pre-teen years, holds his arm and tells him it's going to be okay. No matter what happens, she'll be right there with him. He's afraid of the sharks.

When he tells her, she laughs—no sharks in the river. The song of her laughter propels him forward into darker days.

He's eleven years old when the first plague victim dies. Maia is overseas, studying abroad in London. She's worried she won't be able to come home for Christmas now. Everyone is trying to keep the virus contained. Jay knows nothing about London, but he misses his sister, and he would give anything to be with her again. He packs a bag and tells his parents he's going to the airport, whether they take him or not. He is going to see Maia. They look at each other for a long time, saying nothing. Then, his dad puts him in the car and drives him to get ice cream. As chocolate drips down the side of his cone, he realizes how much his family loves him.

More plague victims die. He isn't sure how old he is when he first understands no one is safe. Maia gets the flu and it's like the sky is falling. His parents hover around the house, gliding in and out of her bedroom, speaking in hushed tones. They're trying to protect him, but the secrets make him sick. She's only able to come back and see them for a few days. She's supposed to go back. He's just praying she survives. When his parents stop talking to him, he pulls his sleeping bag outside her bedroom door.

Jay sleeps until she comes out and tells him she's all right.

He's at the airport, international terminal, and he's saying his goodbyes. Even though the virus is spreading, he wants to be with Maia. Besides, there haven't been any recent outbreaks near the United Kingdom. He's sure he'll be fine. The flight almost gets canceled after someone throws up. When it comes out that a flight attendant is pregnant, everything proceeds as normal. The minute Jay kisses his mom on the cheek, he doesn't know it's the last time he will see her healthy.

He's too young to be jaded and too old to believe in magic. When his father dies, he knows his mother will die, too. Nothing is sacred and no one exempt.

As Jay and Maia look down into the waters of the Thames, he squeezes his sister's hand hard enough to bruise it.

"Ready when you are," he says.

They let the ashes fall.

Chapter Twenty-Two

RUSHING WATER

After the screaming, Jay couldn't talk. He burst into the apartment across the hall and tried to yell for help, but no sound came out. His throat tightened. He stared at Sean, who sat on the couch, until he jumped up and ran over to him.

"Jay," Sean said, "you look awful."

Jay tried to speak again and almost swallowed his tongue. There was no way to put what he was feeling into words. Images of the laboratory flashed in his head—moonlight on the couch, striking Maia's cheek; the bloodshot eyes, unfocused pupils—

Wrong, all wrong.

Sean slapped him. "You're in shock. Take a deep breath. Focus."

There was no pain in his face where Sean had hit him. His whole body was numb—paralyzed, incapable of any kind of feeling.

"Jay," Sean said. "Say something."

Maia's face floated in his mind's eye. Her mouth was open, but she couldn't speak. She'd never speak again.

"Jay, is it Maia?"

She's dead, she's dead, dead, Maia's dead, she's—

Words came out, garbled. "Snap me again."

"*Slap* you, you mean?"

Jay nodded.

Sean's palm collided with his cheek, and once again, he failed to feel it. Still, it cleared his mind.

"Fleur," Jay said.

"What's wrong with the doctor?"

Jay groaned. *It's all Fleur's fault. We left her alone with Maia and now Maia is dead.*

But wait—Fleur hadn't been alone with Maia. Melanie had been there, too.

How had Fleur killed Maia with Melanie around?

"Melanie," Jay said.

"In the bedroom," Sean said. "Think she's looking for pajamas. Once Fleur's out of the bath, Melanie wants a go." He grabbed Jay by the shoulders and jostled him. "That what you were asking? I can't bloody understand you. Tell me what's wrong or else I can't fix it."

He wanted to tell Sean—desperately, in fact—but the words wouldn't come out. His tongue refused to cooperate with the signals in his brain. His body wasn't his.

Sean was in his face, speaking to him again. His eyebrows knit together the way they did when he was worried. Why was he so worried? He wanted to ask Sean what was wrong, but in that moment, he remembered the horror in the room across the hall.

Maia, Maia, Maia. Dead.

"Melanie," he muttered.

"Stay right here. I'll get her."

As if he could move. Jay shifted his weight from one foot to the other with impressive difficulty. He reached up to scratch his nose, but his fingertips were numb. His hands must have fallen asleep.

He rocked his head from side to side to relieve the tension in his neck, but nothing happened.

Everything was numb and he was mute and living in a world where Maia was dead.

Sean came back with Melanie in tow. Judging by the look of panic on her face, Sean had told her something was gravely wrong with Jay.

She took a step toward him and reached out to touch his cheek. He couldn't feel her fingers on his skin, either.

"Sean said you asked for me. What's going on?"

With every ounce of strength he possessed, he pushed the words out.

"Maia, Mels. I… where is Dr. Devereaux? Need to speak with her."

Melanie sighed. "She's in the bath."

"How long?" he asked.

"Dunno," she said. "A while, I think."

"Then why's the tap still running?"

The trio froze and listening to the sound of rushing water breaking through the silence.

Melanie and Sean exchanged puzzled glances.

Water, rushing water full of ashes.

The Thames.

Jay swallowed and tried to keep his knees from going out. "Someone should go see what's going on with her. Need to talk, need to talk, need to talk as soon as possible."

"What's wrong with him?" Melanie asked as though Jay couldn't hear her.

"I think he's in shock, but I'm not sure," Sean said. "At any rate, we need to find out what is going on. Go check on the doctor, see if she's decent."

Melanie went down the hallway and knocked on the bathroom door.

There was no reply, and the water was still running.

"Dr. Devereaux, could I come in? It's only for a moment."

The three of them listened. No response.

Melanie knocked again, harder.

"Dr. Devereaux, are you all right?" She twisted the handle back and forth, swearing and scowling. "Unlock the door, please."

Yet again, the sound of silence punctuated by running water drifted through the apartment.

Melanie waved Sean over to help her. He started by twisting the knob the same way she had. She shot him a look.

"You just saw me try that."

"I dunno," he said.

She put her hands on her hips. "You think you might be strong enough to break this thing down?"

He backed up against the opposite wall and took his time sizing up the door. Jay couldn't break any doors down, even though the one in front of the bathroom looked shoddy at best.

"Can do," Sean said. "Do you think I should?"

Melanie looked back at Jay. He still couldn't move. "Please. He needs help."

Sean dug his left heel into the carpet. He leaned back, raised his right foot, and kicked hard near the lock. The hinges squealed. He kicked again, and the door sprang free.

The minute it was open, there was no going back.

Sean waved at Jay. "Are you coming in with me?"

Jay floated forward toward his friends, unsure of what they'd find.

When Sean broke through the door and it toppled inward, it landed in the middle of an expanding puddle. The puddle was clear fluid punctuated with bright red. Jay scanned it with his eyes, searching for the source. It was coming from the bathtub.

"Jesus Christ," Sean said.

Everything was blood and water.

Melanie screamed and the sound almost shredded Jay's eardrums.

"Get out of here," Sean said. "We've got it. Find Maia."

Melanie bowed her head and disappeared from sight. Jay didn't want her to go looking for Maia, but he was powerless to stop her, paralyzed by fear and awe.

Fleur had left the water running in the tub. It had been running so long it overflowed, spilling over the white lip onto the tile. Water squished under Sean and Jay's feet. Sean yelled at Jay to get back, *stay back, you don't need to see what's in the tub*—Jay took a step forward anyway. When Sean turned off the tap, he told

Jay to get out, go away, don't look at her—but Jay couldn't help himself.

He pushed Sean out of the way and peered into the bathtub. If the floor was a mess, the water was worse.

It was a swirling, angry red that curled around Fleur's limbs and wove itself into her hair. She faced the ceiling, eyes closed. She was still wearing the dress she'd had on earlier—the weight of the water made it cling to her skin. Jay was more disgusted than aroused by the scene.

Like Maia, Fleur's mouth had fallen open.

Unlike Maia, she had cut two trenches in her wrists. With what, he wasn't sure, but she'd done the job well.

"Jesus Christ," Sean said again. "See if she's still breathing."

Jay could only touch her because he was in shock. Because he didn't feel attached to his body, it was easy for him to reach into the water and press his fingers to her neck. The bath was still warm, and the reek of iron mingled with steam made it difficult to focus.

He held his hand against her neck for a few seconds that felt like an eternity.

Nothing close to a pulse fluttered inside her veins.

"No good," Jay said. "She's lost too much blood."

"She just got in," Sean said.

"We were gone a long time. You don't know when she got in."

He put his face in his hands. Jay should have reacted the same way, but he still didn't feel like it.

He didn't feel like anything.

"What are we going to do with her?" Sean asked.

"How am I supposed to know? I'm not the expert on death here."

"Well, neither am I."

Jay looked into the bathtub at Fleur's body again. In the water, she was fragile.

It was impossible to imagine she was the same woman who had smothered his sister with a pillow.

Something tinkled. Jay turned and saw Sean pick up something from under his foot. It was a shard of glass, six inches long, which had come off one of the framed diplomas.

Dark red blood marked the edges of the glass.

"This is our fault," Sean said.

"If she hadn't had the glass, she would've used something else." The sight of the blood had drawn him out of his catatonic state, at least for the time being. The gears of his mind were turning again—slowly, but still turning. "Think about all those pills she had, or the needles. There's always been something."

Sean threw the glass into the sink. It clattered against the side. "I just don't understand why she killed herself. She hadn't seemed depressed. Weren't you two together?"

Jay raised and lowered his shoulders in a shrug. It was the best answer he could give besides the one that wouldn't come; the one he couldn't speak aloud.

I loved her, Sean. I shouldn't have.

"Well," Sean said, "we can't just leave her here. We should bury her or something."

"Where?" Jay asked.

"I don't know, somewhere. Help me carry her out of here."

From the apartment across the hall, there was another scream.

"Maia?" Sean asked.

"Melanie," Jay said. "Maia is dead."

Sean turned the color of milk. He gripped the edge of the sink for support, so he wouldn't collapse beneath the weight of the news.

"The virus, you think?"

"No," Jay said.

Sean ran out of the bathroom to see for himself.

Jay put the lid down on the toilet and sat on it. There was no need for him to see his sister again. He couldn't stomach the sight, especially not when combined with the chaos before him.

Fleur's death was intertwined with Maia's. It was all too horrible for coincidence.

None of it felt real. He kept hoping to wake up, safe in his bed back in London with Samson curled up on his chest.

But that would never happen.

He stood up, determined to search the bathroom for clues. Most people left notes when they killed themselves, didn't they? He wasn't sure when Fleur would've had the time to write one, but he was going to look for it all the same.

He ran his hand under the lip of the tub all the way around, but there was nothing there. Next, he walked over to the sink. The bloody piece of glass had settled on the drain.

He looked up at his reflection and found a piece of paper taped to the mirror instead.

The feeling had come back into his hands. He reached out and took the paper, unfolded it, and started reading before he could find a reason not to.

Chapter Twenty-Three
AN UNSETTLING CROSSROADS

To those left behind, whoever you are,

If you're reading this letter, I have succeeded in one regard and failed in many others. This is my suicide note. At the time I'm writing this, Jay has just relapsed. I thought the treatment was working, but maybe I was wrong. Maybe there is no cure. Maia is dying. The placebo doesn't seem to have made any difference—even in her mind, it's not at all effective. I fear the worst will happen.

I find myself at an unsettling crossroads, caught between the greater good and what I feel in my heart is right. I know I have to keep on doing what I'm doing—it's the only way to move forward— but I'm terrified.

If you never see this letter, it's because I chose to live. It will mean I'm half as brave as I pretend to be. Jay doesn't think anything scares me—we got into an argument about it one time. He asked me what I feared. I couldn't give him a straight answer. I don't even know for sure what I'm afraid of anymore. Every day, it seems like there is something new to fear.

I'm afraid to get too close to Jay. I even tried to kill him while he was in the ice bath. An air bubble in a needle looks just like an act of God, and he would have felt nothing. But I couldn't do it. Instead, for some reason, I told him I loved him. The scariest part is that it wasn't an absolute lie.

Jay is still asleep. I would like to up his dosage. I'm upping Maia's, too. No one else knows it's just sugar. I'm recording everything in the log, but no one will read those notes unless they find a cure. And if someone does discover a cure, they'll be much wiser than me.

I tried curing Jay. When I first met the Harris siblings, I knew one of them would die. Long before I met them, I had made up my mind to stay true to the scientific method when looking for a cure. I knew the experiment wouldn't be valid unless I used a placebo for the control. After all, who cares if someone is cured with one pill if the same results could be achieved without any pill at all? I had to make sure I was doing it right. Everything needed to be perfect if the experiment was going to go off without a hitch.

I can't look Maia in the face when I give her the pills anymore. I can't look at Jay for long, not even when we kiss. I'm finding it more and more difficult to determine what I should and shouldn't do. The further you start in the middle of the gray, the harder it becomes to find the black and white. Still, I know better than to delude myself— my motives were never pure.

When I was sixteen, I fell in love with Auguste, who was in Paris visiting relatives. I met him in the park while riding my bicycle— I ran into a rock and fell off. He managed to catch me, and I was in love. As we sat beneath a tree and he traced circles in my palm, he told me he was from the city of Calais. I hadn't heard much about it. He told me all about it, how beautiful it was, before adding it could never hold a candle to my beauty. I fell too hard, and when the virus took him, no power in heaven or Earth could save me from the fallout. I've never gotten over the pain of losing him.

When I saw Jay, something in his eyes reminded me of Auguste. I wondered if he'd serve as my second chance to save someone. I hadn't been able to rescue Auguste, but maybe somehow I could rescue another. The minute I touched Jay, I made my decision—I'd give Maia the placebo for the sake of saving him. He reminded me of my first love. I didn't expect Jay would soon become my second.

I told him I loved him when I put him in the tub. I doubt he'll remember.

None of that matters.

I'm writing this letter to say I'm sorry. I knew what I did was wrong, but I proceeded anyway, because I am a coward. I know I won't be able to watch Jay and Maia die. The rats are declining, and even that is hard for me. I'm going to kill them so they won't suffer. Jay and Maia, too. And then myself. It's all too much.

I might have been a doctor if I'd never seen the virus. Watching it take so many people out at once without any discretion... it tore me apart. What was the point of saving people when they were still at risk of succumbing to the virus? Instead of helping them recover (as I should have), I used them as participants in my secret trials. When the administration found out, they expelled me and almost put me in prison. I fled Paris and started anew in Calais.

When Jay began responding to the treatment, I was ecstatic. If I discovered a cure, I could go back to Paris. I could finish my studies. I could earn my degree—I wouldn't have to fake it. No one would care how the experiments happened if they helped destroy the virus. I would be a hero.

Since Jay relapsed, I'm starting to see how foolish I've been, how careless. If you're reading this letter, it's because I've taken my own life. I've killed Jay, Maia, or both. The guilt is overwhelming. I'm not asking for forgiveness. I know I don't deserve it. The four of you made me want to be a better person. I'm sorry I failed you.

Au revoir.

—Fleur

The next morning, the trio was up with the sun. With the gurney, they moved Fleur and Maia's bodies from the apartment to the street. There was a big church with a graveyard a couple blocks away. Maia deserved a proper burial. Maybe Fleur didn't, but she'd get one, anyway.

He showed Fleur's letter to Sean and Melanie. Neither of them had known what to say. She'd made herself out to be a martyr, but they all knew the truth. After all, they had *known* her—Jay more so than anyone else.

When they finished reading it, Jay ripped the letter to shreds and let it fall out of a window and off into the world.

Au revoir.

As the three of them carried the bodies to church, Jay couldn't help wishing they had a casket. He didn't like the idea of just digging a hole and dropping his sister in the ground. Somehow, it was wrong. Maybe Fleur deserved that, but Maia didn't.

He also wished he'd managed to prepare a eulogy. Even a few points, scribbled on a piece of paper, would've been better than nothing. At his parents' funeral, he regretted not speaking for them. His head was full of memories of a happy childhood and a civil adolescence. He'd been blessed with great parents; he wanted everyone to know. But once he saw the urns nestled in the casket, everything he had to say vanished from his mind. Maia couldn't speak, either. Grief had muted them. And now, he had regrets. So many regrets.

Sean had told Jay once that he'd spoken at all his family's funerals. Although it had been difficult getting through the speeches, Sean was happy he'd done it. Reflecting on his loved ones' lives gave Sean a closure Jay envied.

He still couldn't believe Maia wasn't waking up. In death, she seemed at peace. Melanie had wiped the dried blood off Maia's face. She looked like she had before Fleur smothered her. She'd been so sick that her skin, in death, didn't look much different than when she was alive.

Sean had volunteered to maneuver the gurney. Melanie held one side of it to help steer. Jay felt relieved he didn't have to walk right next to them. When he caught a glimpse of Maia, his chest cavity collapsed. The less he looked at her, the better.

No one said a word until they reached the cemetery. Sean stopped the gurney, and Melanie took one of the shovels Jay had been carrying.

He held the other against his chest. "What're you doing?"

"Digging," she answered. "Give that one to Sean."

When Jay didn't move, Sean reached out and wrapped his hand around the handle of the shovel. "Let us do this for you, mate. It would be an honor."

Jay handed the shovel over.

Sean and Melanie walked to an empty plot of landed, rested their blades against the dirt, and waited. Jay's stomach twisted. He would have to move the gurney with the bodies over to the plot. He didn't know if he could do it.

Sean leaned on his shovel. "Hang on."

"I can do it." The words surprised him even though they came from his own mouth. If he wanted closure, he'd have to accept the reality of Maia's death and burial. The easiest way to do that would be to interact.

He wrapped his fingers around the cold metal handle and pulled the gurney forward. The uneven soil shifted with each step he took. When he arrived at the grave, he stopped. Unbidden, his eyes focused on his sister's body, and his stomach lurched again.

It wasn't his sister. It wasn't Maia; no, not anymore. It was just the shell of what his sister had once been. She wasn't in pain or unhappy where she was. She'd been set free. No matter how the burial went, she was already gone. She was with his parents now, and they would take good care of her.

He'd always heard that funerals existed for the living. For the first time in his life, Jay thought he understood.

Sean and Melanie made quick work of digging a hole. It was their way of honoring Maia. Every time they moved the dirt, they were proving they loved her. Jay's eyes filled with tears.

He hadn't let himself cry yet. Until the moment they broke ground, he'd still been in shock.

The rest of the burial passed in a blur. Sean and Melanie, together, put Fleur's body in the ground. Melanie clicked her tongue as she threw dirt in the hole. He felt like he should say something, but he couldn't—not for Fleur. After everything she'd done, he wouldn't let himself waste a single word on her. It sickened him to think of all the time he'd spent with her. He could've spent that time taking care of his sister. If only he'd known, everything would have been different. Maybe then Fleur wouldn't have needed to kill her. Was it his fault she was dead?

I'm sorry, Maia. So sorry I failed.

Once they covered Fleur's body, Sean smoothed the surface of the dirt with his shovel. He looked back over his shoulder at Jay, keeping his gaze far away from the gurney. There was only one body left for them to bury now.

"Take a moment if you need it," Sean said. "Just tell us when you're ready. Take all the time you need."

Melanie smiled. "Do you want to be alone?"

"No," Jay said, "never."

He needed them there. The memories were coming, and he couldn't face them on his own. Jay needed to embrace them, but only with his friends.

"We're here for you," said Melanie.

"Forever, mate," Sean added.

Jay pulled the salty air into his lungs. It all came rushing back without much conscious effort. He thought back over the past several weeks to the day he'd found Maia in his apartment. Hunched over the sink, retching and bloody, he swore he'd never let anything happen to her. Although he hadn't kept his promise, she'd forgiven him. Her love was unconditional, even in death. He knew she didn't blame him for what had happened to her. She'd died still thinking he was the best brother in the world. He'd cling to that thought until he didn't need it anymore. He didn't know when that would be, but it would happen. He was counting on it.

Jay slipped a hand into his pocket and closed his fingers around his mother's necklace. He drew strength from the smooth metal of the heart-shaped charm. If memory served, he and Maia had pooled their money to buy the jewelry for Mother's Day one year. In reality, Maia had most likely paid for the whole thing. Still, she had let Jay take some of the credit.

Without a word, Jay took the necklace out of his pocket and fastened it around his sister's neck. The metal was warmer than her skin. He brushed his palm over her forehead, pushing the hair off her pallid face. His eyes flickered over her one last time before he kissed her cheek.

An overwhelming peace settled over Jay then. Melanie and Sean were staring at him.

"I'm ready," he said. "Let's lay her to rest."

He wasn't ready, but he had to be. It was time to let her go.

When Sean and Melanie lowered Maia into the grave, Jay chose not to look at her. He wanted to remember the Maia he'd grown up with. He closed his eyes, and she was smiling there, laughing and teasing him like she always had. In his memories, his sister would live on forever—as healthy and as happy as she deserved to be.

The dam behind his eyes broke after his friends had finished. His eyes, nose, and throat burned with the release of so much tension. Had he ever cried so much before? Did it even matter then?

Melanie was the first to lay her shovel down. She took Jay's hand in hers and pressed her cheek against his shoulder. Sean gave them a moment to stand with each other. When the time was right, he put his shovel down, too, and grabbed Jay's other hand. The three of them stood looking into the grave silhouetted forms against a rising yellow sun. One family was lost, but another had replaced it.

The ache inside his chest would likely disappear with time.

ABOUT THE AUTHOR

Briana Morgan is a young adult author and freelance editor who loves dark, suspenseful reads, angst-ridden relationships, and complicated characters. Her interest in Jay Gatsby scares her friends and family. You can find her in way too many places online, eating too much popcorn, reading in the corner, or crying about long-dead literary heroes. You can visit her website at *www.brianamorganbooks.com*. She currently resides somewhere near Atlanta, Georgia.

Made in the USA
Columbia, SC
03 January 2021

30241660R00109